Wading Through
Peanut Butter

Other Apple Paperbacks you will enjoy:

Wading Through Peanut Butter

Pamela Curtis Swallow

AN
APPLE
PAPERBACK

SCHOLASTIC INC.
New York Toronto London Auckland Sydney

To my mother and
in memory of my father,
who, during their years in education,
have helped more than one Bently
wade through.

ACKNOWLEDGMENTS

Sincere thanks to Paula Danziger
for her support, wisdom, and humor.

ISBN 0-590-45793-4

12 11 10 9 8 7 6 5 4 3 2 1   3 4 5 6 7 8/9

Printed in the U.S.A.   28

First Scholastic printing, December 1993

1.
Hey, Who's That?

It was a direct hit. *Splat*. A steamroller couldn't have done it better.

"Oops," I said, lifting Howard's flattened lunch bag off the green vinyl seat. The school bus had lurched ahead just as I was sitting down. "Sorry. The driver could have waited a little before taking off like that."

Howard nodded and examined his squashed bag. Peanut butter oozed out one end.

"Looks pretty bad," I said. Howard Funstein was my best friend, and that was his first lunch of the school year I had just wrecked. It was the only homemade lunch Howard would get all year. After the first day, his parents always gave him money to buy lunch, no matter what was on the menu — even fish patties.

"At least I've finally discovered my special talent," I said, grinning. "Flattening sandwiches. I did a great job."

"Congratulations, Bently, but do it on *yours* next time," Howard said.

"I'll switch with you. Peanut butter's my favorite, anyway, even squished." I looked out the bus window. For the first time I was actually excited about starting school. It was going to be great. This year I knew just what I'd find there, what to expect. I liked that.

Last year had been awful. First I'd had Mrs. Newman for a teacher, but she left in January to have a baby. Then Mr. Wilson took over. He never corrected, or even handed back, any papers. In five weeks, he was gone. Our class finished the year with Mrs. Skullifino, better known as The Screaming Skull, who acted as if it had been all our fault that the other teachers hadn't lasted. Last spring with her was a Guinness Record Book headache.

"Hey," Howard said. "What's that black-and-blue mark on your chin?"

"Oh, it's from my sister. She can't take a joke."

"Seven out of ten sisters can't — what kind of joke?"

I smiled. "Well, I was awake for a long time last night — couldn't get to sleep. I was bored, so I decided to stir up a little excitement."

"Yeah? What'd you do?"

"I took two flashlights, crept down to Colleen's room, then charged in, yelling, 'TRUCK!' She

2

screamed, swung her arms at the flashlights, and knocked one of them into my face."

"Ouch." Howard winced. "Guess she punched your lights out."

"Definitely," I agreed.

"Didn't your parents get mad at you?" Howard asked.

"They just yelled at me to get back to my room."

Howard sighed happily and leaned back in his seat. "We finally made it, Bent — fifth grade." He wrinkled his nose to get his glasses to move up.

"Yup. Mrs. Evans's class . . . at last," I said. Mrs. Evans was the best teacher in the school. Two years ago my sister had been in her class. Mrs. Evans used to tell me that she liked my red hair and that she looked forward to having me in her room.

"Remember how big the fifth graders seemed two years ago? And remember their field trips," I said, "and the dry ice Mrs. Evans brought in for a science experiment? That was cool."

"Yeah. Ice usually is — but, hey, did you know that you can actually get burned touching dry ice?"

"Nope."

Howard went on about dry ice, but I wasn't listening. I had other things to think about.

Ahhh, the year was going to be great. I'd stand out, maybe even be outstanding. After all, my teacher already knew me and liked me. I wasn't going to be just an average fifth grader walking into the classroom. I'd have a head start. It was my year, and I knew it. Soon, when I walked down the hall, kids would say, "There goes Bently Barker . . . WOW!"

I touched the window. "Hey, I know this window. I stuck this Chiquita banana sticker on the glass."

"That's right. We were in this same seat when you nearly threw up last spring. Remember?" Howard grinned. "Yecchhh."

I nodded. "Yeah, well, I *didn't*, so 'yecchhh' yourself." I flicked off the baseball hat that Howard wore perched on top of his curly dark hair. Howard punched me in the shoulder.

Howard had stayed right with me that day I'd felt sick. Only a really good friend would stay in his seat when the person next to him was all set to throw up.

The bus bounced along, stopped to let on kids, and bounced on again. Most were dressed better than they would be the rest of the year. Howard and I both had on new jeans, and Howard had new sneakers. My mom said we'd shop for my sneakers after school.

Maureen Hiffard got on the bus. I was sure I saw little Louie Schmidt cringe as she got close.

She tweaked Louie's head as she went by.

Maureen plunked down in the seat behind Howard and me. I heard a groan and wasn't sure if it was Howard or the bus seat.

"So," Maureen said, leaning close to our ears, "room sixteen?"

I heard the groan again. It wasn't the seat. In fact, now it was a two-boy groan, coming from Howard and Louie.

"Yup," I answered.

"I knew it." She sighed loudly and leaned back. "Every year I've got you guys in my class — Bently Barfer, Howard Fungus, and Louie Smidgen."

Howard rolled his eyes. "Maureen hasn't gotten any nicer over the summer," he whispered. "I heard she put Louie in the trash can at the park."

"Look at her. Why is she growing faster than we are?" I whispered. "She's catching up to Anthony Magliari." Anthony was a legend in the school — he was the biggest seventh grader in the world.

"Howard, are we midgets or what? We're runty next to her."

"We may look shrimpy now, but we'll grow. It's a fact of life. Boys grow later than girls," said Howard.

"What if we don't grow?"

"We can always lift weights — you know, pump iron — and build up our bodies," Howard pointed

5

out. "Seven out of ten males do that, you know."

I tried to imagine Howard and Louie and me with big, puffed-up muscles. I smiled and looked out the window as the bus pulled into the school driveway. Maybe with Mrs. Evans, we'd be so busy taking field trips and doing experiments, Maureen wouldn't have time to bother us.

Howard and I hurried down the hall, then stopped short as we got close to room sixteen. "Hey, who's that? Where's Mrs. Evans?" I gasped. The short, chubby man standing by the classroom door definitely wasn't Mrs. Evans.

Howard shrugged. "A substitute? This has to be Mrs. Evans's room. Number sixteen is always hers."

As we got to the room, I stepped back to check the name and room number over the door. "I don't believe this. Whose name is that?" I was getting a terrible feeling. I was all set for Mrs. Evans. Why wasn't she all set for me?

2.
Mr. Corby

"**H**i, I'm Mr. Corby. Welcome to fifth grade," the man said. He smiled. "Look around, choose a desk, and get ready for an interesting year."

"He doesn't sound much like a substitute," I whispered as I dropped my backpack on the floor and kicked it under a desk. What was going on? Whoever this man was, I wished he'd get out of Mrs. Evans's room.

Howard was looking toward one corner of the room. "Hey, Bent," he said. "Look at those tanks!"

Louie followed us as we hurried toward the two aquarium tanks sitting on top of a bookshelf. One tank had water in it, the other didn't.

"Ahhh . . . looks like a Gila monster in this one." Howard scroonched his glasses, looking into the dry tank. "No, wait — maybe not. Looks like an iguana. Great!"

"Oohh, my gosh . . ." exclaimed Louie. "It's HUGE."

A sign on the tank read JUGHEAD.

I stared at Jughead. I'd seen wiggly rubber reptiles that looked better.

"You won't believe this, guys," Howard said, stretching to see the back part of the other tank. "I think I see an octopus behind that rock."

"Come on." I leaned over to look. "Could be just seaweed."

"I don't think anyone would name a piece of seaweed 'Archie.' " Howard pointed to the sign.

"Oohh, my gosh . . ." Louie said again. "Wait'll my mom hears about this. I'm allergic to shrimp. I wonder if I'm allergic to these things, too?"

"Oh, get real, Lou." Howard said, wiggling his fingers in Louie's face.

"No, seriously. Remember last year when Maria brought in her hamster? I sneezed the whole time it was near me." Louie glanced around the room. "I wonder what else is here? Probably the Loch Ness Monster lurking in another tank."

"This teacher's into signs, and there's none that says 'Nessie,' " Howard said. "You're safe."

A lot of other kids were in the room now, claiming desks and talking to each other. Lisa Rogers walked in. She looked at me, smiled, and gave a little wave. Suddenly my ears felt weird, as if they were turning red.

A few kids noticed the tanks. "Hey! What's in those?" Willie Albert asked.

"Let *me* see," Maureen said, barging in between Andy Ogden and Willie. She marched up to the tanks, looked in, then backed away. "Blaghh!"

That "blaghh!" got everyone's attention.

"Eeuuuw!" said Maureen's friend Audrey.

"Awww right! Awesome!" Andy and Willie shouted.

There was such a stampede of kids, I thought I was going to get trampled.

"All right, everyone, take your seats." Mr. Corby stood there with his roll book in his hand. He seemed to be one of those tricky people who could smile and be tough at the same time. Everyone quickly sat.

Since Howard had been busy looking around when he came in, he had to take what was left, a desk between the Mason twins. "Okay if I sit here, or do you two want to sit together?" Howard asked.

"You can sit there," they said, sounding like twin stereo speakers.

He looked like a Howard sandwich, on twin bread — Peggy on the left, Patty on the right. I was on the other side of Peggy.

Howard opened his desk and put his baseball hat inside. Then he leaned across his desk toward me. "It doesn't matter where we sit now, Bent. Teachers just say to pick a seat, but then they move you where they want you."

I watched Howard unpack his backpack. He was the only kid to bring a pile of books on the first day of school: a dictionary, an almanac, *The Guinness Book of World Records*, some nature guides, sports books. He liked to be ready for on-the-spot research.

My desk was nothing like Howard's. It always ended up being a black hole, where things would disappear — math papers I didn't want to take home, library books, library overdue notices, old floppy carrot sticks, moldy fruit. . . .

Mr. Corby cleared his throat and hiked up his pants. "Okay, gang. Now that we're settled, let's get started."

Willie leaned over and whispered to Andy. They'd been best friends since first grade and even had the same short buzz haircuts.

"You want to say something?" Mr. Corby asked Willie.

"Uh — we thought Mrs. Evans was our teacher," Willie said. He scratched his neck the way he always did when he talked to teachers.

"Mrs. Evans moved over the summer. I was hired to replace her," Mr. Corby answered.

I sagged in my seat. It was definite. No Mrs. Evans. How could she do this? Didn't she remember she was going to have me in her class? Didn't she know that Mr. Corby might not work out, and we could end up with The Screaming Skull again?

"Mrs. Evans must have found out that Willie was going to be in her class. That's why she quit," Andy said, grinning at Willie. Willie made a face back.

Mr. Corby smiled and shook his head. "Not quite. I was told it was a family matter." He jiggled a piece of chalk in his hand as he spoke. "I also heard that she's on an archeological dig somewhere out west right now. Hey, who knows, maybe she'll send us a fossil." He hiked up his pants again.

Howard smiled.

I wondered what Howard was smiling about — the fossil, or the way Mr. Corby kept hiking up his pants.

Mr. Corby said a few more things that teachers always say on the first day. I wondered if messages like "Thou shalt not let thy students go to the bathroom without permission," and "Thou shalt drink coffee and have coffee breath," come flashing out of the sky when people make up their minds to become teachers. Mr. Corby had a thermos on his desk and a coffee stain on his tie.

There was more of Mr. Corby in the front than in the back. I guess that was why he was having trouble keeping his pants up.

When I heard Mr. Corby say, "I want you to tell me about yourselves," I started to pay attention again. I was either going to have to write or talk. I wished I had a third choice — vaporize.

It wasn't supposed to be like this. So much for knowing what to expect, for being the kid with a head start. What a way to begin fifth grade.

Mr. Corby continued. "Since I'm asking you to tell me something about you, it's only fair that I should tell you something about me. Okay. Let's see . . ." He tossed up the piece of chalk he'd been holding and caught it. "Well . . . my favorite activity is scuba diving. My favorite thing to eat is black licorice. And . . . I like science and animals. . . ."

That last one wasn't hard to figure out. Besides Jughead and Archie, there were shells, a bird's nest, and a pile of something that looked like cow poop, but had to be something better — maybe lava.

"I have some unusual pets," Mr. Corby went on.

I heard Howard whisper that octopi have poisonous saliva. Louie murmured, "Oohh, my gosh . . ."

"Maybe I'll bring in a few others one day," Mr. Corby said.

"Like what?" Louie squeaked.

"Oh, a tarantula, a boa . . ."

There were a lot of excited comments from the

class. Louie just kept saying, "Oohh, my gosh . . . oohh, my gosh."

"Okay . . . what else can I tell you?" Mr. Corby continued. "I also like writing. We'll let our creative juices flow."

I wasn't exactly sure what Mr. Corby meant about creative juices. Maybe it was the opposite of poisonous saliva.

"Now . . . what are things I don't like? Hmm . . ." He tossed the chalk up a few more times. "I don't like standing in long lines. I don't like neckties," said Mr. Corby, whipping off his wrinkled one. "And I *don't* like having dessert at the end of the meal." He winked at the class. "I say — begin with it!"

Maybe he won't be so bad, I thought. Maybe he could put in a good word for desserts when he talks to the parents at Meet-the-Teacher Night. And maybe he'll explain what that poopy-looking pile is.

"Now, it's your turn. Write about the things *you* like and don't like," said Mr. Corby as he passed out paper. "Don't worry about handwriting or spelling today. We'll deal with that later. Just tell me about yourselves."

"How many things should we tell?" Louie asked.

"About the amount I told you," Mr. Corby said. "Or more, if you want."

While I was trying to figure out how much I

had to write, I could see Howard smiling. He had gotten over his disappointment about Mrs. Evans and was eager to tell about himself.

But how far should I go with this "like and don't like" thing?

3.
Goals

Things I like —
          by Bently Barker

1) Opening a new box of cereal
   before my sister gets it
2) Jujubes — the little candies
   that stick to your teeth
3) Collections — like stickers off
   bananas, weird pens, and
   moths that die under the
   porch light
4) Snow days
5) Frozen grapes with a glob
   of peanut butter on top
6) Pets — Farful, my dog
            Katie, my cat
            Ruckles, my turtle

I like the way pets act glad
to see you when you come home.
It's a little hard to see a turtle
act glad, but if you know him,
you can. Pets usually act extra
nice if your day wasn't so great.

I stared at my paper and thought about telling Mr. Corby that I liked knowing what to expect, and that I had liked that I'd practically been guaranteed a chance to stand out and be special in fifth grade. I began to write it, then erased. Then started over, and erased. Finally I left it off for good. It wasn't Mr. Corby's fault that Mrs. Evans had left.

Things I don't like —
       by Bently Barker

1) Surprises with poisonous saliva.

I erased that and started again:

1) My sister's curling iron and makeup all over the bathroom
2) Spelling-list stories
3) Baked beans, when the juice oozes onto my hot-dog roll
4) Smelly feet
5) Orange juice — I don't trust it. Once I drank some chicken fat that my mom had put into an orange juice carton
6) Helium balloons in my bedroom

I wondered if Mr. Corby would understand that last one. Balloons sometimes give me the creeps. I don't like the way they seem to follow me around the house. One night, two "Happy Birthday" balloons with grinny faces lowered themselves over my head. When I woke up the next morning, they were an inch above my nose.

I glanced across Peggy's paper to see how Howard was doing. He had put down his pencil and was reading one of his books from home. I leaned over to read what Howard had written. He'd put down that he liked reading, computers, being soccer goalie, and science fiction movies.

On his list of things he didn't like, Howard had put: the smell of shrimp cooking, sand in his bed, and *The Dating Game* show on TV that his sister and her friends watched. He walked around his house gagging whenever it was on.

While I was staring at Lisa Rogers and wondering what she was writing, Mr. Corby cleared his throat to get everyone's attention. "As you're finishing up, I'm going to be handing out something else." He held up a stack of blue softcover composition books.

Arrgghh. The last time a teacher gave me a book like that, I was supposed to fill it with all the math facts I'd messed up on. My book was jam-packed.

"I'll explain," Mr. Corby said as he walked

around the room putting a book on each desk. "Driving to school this morning, I asked myself, 'Warren, what would you like to see happen this year?' "

Warren, I'd like to see Bently Barker get all A's and be the most outstanding fifth grader of all time, I thought.

Mr. Corby paused for a moment, then walked to the blackboard and wrote GOALS in big letters. "What does this word mean?"

"It's what you get in soccer when Howard is goalie and he's too busy reading to notice you kicking the ball past him," Andy called out.

With his nostrils flared, Howard gave Andy a squinty-eyed glare. But it was true about his reading on the field. That's why he liked soccer — he could read while he played it. When the ball wasn't near the goal, he would take a book out of his back pocket. Then he'd read until the ball got close. Sometimes *too* close.

Mr. Corby smiled. "You're thinking of goals in a sport. But okay, that ties in with what I'm getting at."

Howard's hand went up. "A goal can mean something you're working for. A purpose." Howard turned to Andy and whispered, "Hah," then he opened his desk and reached for a book. "One minute, Mr. Corby. I'll give you an exact definition. . . ."

Mr. Corby laughed. "No need. You're right on

target. Goals give us direction. Goals give us something to shoot for."

I was getting uneasy. What was he getting at? Who needed help with his goals? Warren? Didn't he know what he was doing? Weren't teachers supposed to know those things? Uh-oh. Was I on a ship without a captain? A plane without a pilot? A carousel without a horse? Were we going to end up with The Screaming Skull again?

"I set a couple of goals for myself this year," Mr. Corby went on.

Good, I thought.

"And I will soon be sharing my goals with you. But for now, what I'd like you to do is think about a goal for yourself," Mr. Corby said. "What would you like to see happen this year? You don't have to decide on one right away. Take some time."

"Is this homework?" Audrey asked.

"No, not unless you want to do it at home. But some of you might want to," Mr. Corby answered. He gave his pants a tug. "Sometime, between now and Friday afternoon, you should write your goal in your book."

"Does this count?" asked Maureen. "For a grade?"

Mr. Corby shook his head. "You don't even have to show me what you wrote, if you don't want to. It can be a secret goal that no one else has to know about."

"But it doesn't count?" she repeated.

"Not the way you're thinking. But it's important, and after a while, as we get to know each other better, some of you may want to share your goals."

Maureen looked pleased that it didn't count.

"How long?" asked Louie.

"Until it's done," Mr. Corby answered.

More teacher stuff. They all say that.

"All right, I'll give you a couple more minutes to finish up," Mr. Corby said. "Then we'll get on with our day."

As I began to think about my goal, I smiled. I had a head start in this class after all. It wasn't the head start I'd expected, but I did, at least, already have a goal. Maybe it could still be a great year. And maybe I wouldn't be just an average fifth grader.

I jumped as I heard Peggy yell. Her eyes were open really wide. She was staring at the aquariums.

"Patty, look!" She reached around Howard, poked her twin in the shoulder, and pointed to the corner.

I looked. My stomach lurched. So did something from Archie's tank. It looked like part of Archie. But it was bigger than I thought any of Archie's parts should be. "Uh-oh."

"Huh?" Howard said. He looked at the tank. The long tentacle was stretching over the top. "Wow! He's getting out!"

4.
Bently Barker,
Average Fifth Grader

Without thinking, I leaped from my seat. Somewhere between my way up from the chair and my way down to the floor, the thinking began. Running away from Archie would be chickenhearted. Running toward Archie would be brave. I could be a hero on the first day of school. I'd be set for the rest of the year . . . Bently the Lionhearted!

As I started toward the tank, I felt myself falling forward. The toe of my sneaker was caught in the shoulder strap of my backpack on the floor. Instead of soaring, Superman style, to save the day, I fell flat, flounder style.

Lying stupidly, nose to the floor, I waited for the laughter and the remarks. There was plenty of noise, but not aimed at me. I looked up in time to see Mr. Corby hustle across the room. In a flash he stuffed Archie back into the tank.

Hoping no one noticed me, I got up and quietly slipped back into my seat.

"Are you okay?" Peggy asked.

"Graceful move," Maureen commented. "A bit *bent* out of shape, huh, *Bent*ly?"

I turned red. On the good side, only two people noticed. On the bad side, one of them was Maureen.

"There," Mr. Corby said firmly as the class watched him hitch a metal latch to the lid. "Archie Houdini, the escape artist, is not getting out."

Howard, Louie, and I sat in a three-seater on the way home on the bus. "Boy, did you see how fast Mr. Corby took off across the room to catch Archie?" Howard said. "Wish I'd had a stopwatch on him."

"Mr. Corby is the fastest human in history to wrestle a six-foot creature back into its tank," Louie added.

"As usual, you exaggerate, Lou," Howard said.

Neither Howard nor Louie said anything about my bellyflop. That was one good thing about still being average. People don't watch you much.

"What if he'd gotten all the way out?" Louie asked. "And what if he'd stretched out one of his nasty, long arms and strangled someone? Or zapped someone with his poison saliva? Could've been me. I'm *sure* I'd be allergic to *that* stuff."

"You should have been named Louie 'What If' Schmidt," Howard teased. "Nine out of ten kids who say, 'What if' have mothers who also say, 'What if.' "

"My mother doesn't say, 'What if,' she says, 'When,' " Louie answered. Unless she had some sort of medical condition or worry to think about, Louie's mother wasn't happy. She carried a spray can of Lysol around in her purse. I'd seen her disinfect playground equipment before letting Louie on it.

"I had a Rubberman toy once that stretched like Archie," I said. "It was creepy."

"Yeah, mine stretched twenty feet," Louie added.

"Like all your stories, Louie," Howard said quietly.

"Well, I just hope Mr. Corby keeps that lid locked," Louie said. "What if Archie could break the lock?"

"Archie probably listened to all that stuff about having goals, you know. His is to get out," I said, laughing.

"Wrong, an octopus has no ears," Howard corrected me.

"That's his other goal — to have ears," I said.

"So," Howard said, rolling his eyes and moving on to a new subject, "what do you think about Mr. Corby?"

I pulled a linty orange Jujube out of my pocket and popped it into my mouth. "Warren?

Mmmm — he's okay, but not what I was expecting."

"Yeah . . . but I think he might be even better than okay. So, you know what my goal's going to be?" Howard asked.

"Mine's to grow," Louie said, sitting up taller.

I stuck my finger in my mouth and poked the Jujube off my tooth, and waited for Howard to tell his goal.

"I want to get through volume 'H' in my *World Book Encyclopedia*."

"You mean you just read that for *fun*? Every bit?"

"Yup."

"Don't they add new stuff every year?" Louie asked. "Aren't you afraid you'll miss something?"

Howard shrugged. "Nope. I get the yearbooks and keep up-to-date with those."

I was glad Howard and Louie hadn't asked me about my goal. I'd written it, but I wasn't ready to tell it.

MY GOAL —
     by Bently Barker

I want to be outstanding, not boring. When other kids think of me, I want them to go, "wow!"

But it was hard to feel outstanding when every school year began the same way. The class would get divided into reading and math groups and it was always the same — Bently in the middle. The high group got to go down the hall to meet with a special teacher. The low group got to go up the hall to work with another special teacher. But the middle group just stayed put and plodded along without even changing seats.

Lisa Rogers was in the high group. I wondered if she'd notice me — Bently Barker, average fifth grader, the kid who practically never got out of his seat . . . except to fall.

Just once I would like to hear a teacher say, "Okay class, it's time for Group One to get out the multiplication fact papers, and for Group Two to go see Ms. Lovemath, and for Bently Barker to take his private taxi to the Albert Einstein Institute for Outstanding Kids."

5.
Frog Feet

"Hi, Bently. How was your first day?" my mom asked, opening the front door. Farful wagged her hind end as she greeted me, and Katie hopped down from the windowsill, arched her back, and strolled my way.

"It was okay." I scratched Farful behind her ears, then scooped up Katie. "We have an iguana and an octopus in our class, and a new teacher."

"Your voice got a little muffled in Katie's fur. It sounded like you said you have an iguana and an octopus for teachers," Mom said, laughing.

"Not exactly," I answered, setting Katie down.

"Mrs. Evans is into animals this year?" Mom asked as we walked into the kitchen.

"Not exactly." I sat down at the table.

"Not exactly again? Bently, what do you mean, 'not exactly'?"

"I mean I don't have Mrs. Evans. I have a new teacher, Warren Corby." It was kind of fun using a teacher's first name.

She looked surprised. "Corby? What happened? You were assigned to Mrs. Evans's room."

"Well, I got her room. But she's not in it."

Mom looked puzzled.

"She moved."

"Ohhh . . . well, what's the new teacher like?"

I shrugged. "Warren's okay."

Mom laughed. "I'm sure Warren will be fine, although he probably prefers that you call him Mr. Corby. Do your books look interesting?"

The only things I see when I flip through new school books are all the questions I'm going to have to answer. "I don't know. I'm still in the middle groups, Mom. Just average."

"You, average? Never."

Easy for her to say. She and the rest of the family have *had* high-group minds. I should have inherited one.

Mom teaches history at the community college in our town. She knows more names and dates than anyone I know. On family vacations she always finds museums and monuments.

Dad writes computer programs and computer books. I'm sure he's a genuine genius.

My sister, Colleen, doesn't know report cards even come with anything but A's on them. She has no problems in school, except ones that have to do with boys. As far as I can tell, the only thing Colleen is bad at is singing — and what's weird is that Colleen is positive she's going to be a famous singer, star of stage and video. I don't see how that could ever happen — her voice is terrible.

My family's not average, so why am I?

I stood up and started opening cupboard doors to look for a snack. I have a habit of checking the same cupboard three or four times. It's as if I believe that goodies could mysteriously sprout up between peeks. "What's to eat?"

"There are peanut butter cookies in the jar, and there's cider."

Peanut butter cookies — my favorite. Between bites I said, "We're going shopping, right? For my sneakers?"

"We don't have to after all," she said, grinning.

That was good news. I don't like to shop.

"When I was out this morning, I looked in the sneaker place. Colleen had seen some high-tops she wanted." Mom walked to the counter and picked up a bag. "There was a special sale. If I bought two pairs, the second pair cost only one dollar. So I found the ones Colleen wanted and got you a pair, too."

"Let's see," I said. I liked new sneakers.

Mom reached in the bag. She pulled out a pair of white high-tops. "Ta-da! These are Colleen's." Then she held up a pair of pea-green low-tops. "Ta-da! These are yours. Pretty slick, don't you think?"

I did not like *those* new sneakers. There was

probably only one pair of ugly green sneakers like that in the entire world. My mother found them and bought them for *me*.

"They're a size bigger than your old ones, so you won't grow out of them for a while. What do you think?" She dangled them.

I blinked my eyes slowly, hoping the sneakers would be gone when I looked again. They weren't. "A frog would like them, Mom." Would a girl like Lisa ever like a guy with Kermit-the-frog feet?

"Oh, dear. I sense that you don't love them," she said. "We have a small problem. All sales were final. We can't return them."

I groaned. "Mom — you can't expect me to wear those."

"Bently, I was trying to save time and money. I'm sorry these aren't what you want." She brushed some crumbs off the table into her hand and then let them drop into the garbage. "I don't believe in wasting perfectly good sneakers, though, and I really don't have time now to run out for others. Once you've worn them a few times, you'll get used to them. They'll be all right until we can do something about them later."

"No way will I put those on," I muttered. "I'd rather wear the sneaker boxes than those gross things. We have to get a normal pair *soon* . . . *very soon* . . . before everyone thinks I'm a total weirdo."

I trudged upstairs carrying my new sneakers

and grumbling. "This is what I get for wanting to stand out — average sneakers would have been good, but now I've got outstandingly ugly ones." I should have made my goal clearer.

Before going to bed, I pulled my goal book out of my backpack. I looked at the goal I'd written earlier, then below it, I wrote:

MY GOAL — PART TWO

I want to be known for my outstanding feats, not my outstanding feet.

6.
Camouflage Sneakers

In the morning, I couldn't find my old sneakers. Major panic. "Mom, where are my sneakers?" I yelled down the stairs.

"They're in the box. By your closet door."

I looked toward the closet. "I mean the old ones," I yelled down again. "The new ones aren't broken in yet." Maybe she'd think I had to do something special to them to get them ready to wear. What I wanted to do was junk them.

"Bently, stop yelling," screamed Colleen. "I can't hear myself sing." She was in the bathroom. How could she not hear herself sing? The rest of the neighborhood could. Even Farful couldn't take it. She was under my bed with her paws over her ears.

Mom stood at the bottom of the stairs and called up, "I figured your old sneakers were shot. They're out in the trash."

"Oh, no! Mom, I need them. Have the garbage men come yet?"

31

"Haven't heard them," she answered.

I dashed down the stairs, scooted past her, and ran outside barefoot. The garbage cans were on the sidewalk. As I lifted the lid off the first one, the smell of spoiled coleslaw filled my nose. "Yuck!" I slammed the lid back on, hoping my sneakers would be resting neatly at the top in the other can.

Standing back, with my head turned, I lifted the second lid and waited for the smell to ease up. Then I looked in. There they were. I could see the laces of one and the toe of the other. But they weren't resting neatly on top. They were covered with stinky, used cat litter. "Oh, brother." I let the lid drop.

I ran back inside and up the stairs two at a time. Colleen was still belting out "I'd Like to Teach the World to Sing" in the bathroom. What a horrible thought — Colleen teaching the world to sing the way she did.

I snuck into her room, picked up her telephone, and dialed. "Howard? Emergency. Meet me behind your garage in ten minutes. And bring that can of spray paint you used on that model B–17 bomber."

Panting, I leaned against the back wall of Howard's garage and waited. He was probably still at the breakfast table, chewing. His mom had a thing about not eating fast. Howard had to chew every bite ten times before he swallowed. She even made me do that when I ate at their house.

Finally I heard the door slam, and Howard came around the side of the building. I could see he had some breakfast stored in his cheeks.

"You got the paint?" I asked.

Howard pulled the can out from under his sweater and held it up. "For the last ten minutes I have been trying to figure out what you want with this, 'specially since you called the color 'caterpillar-guts green.' "

"It's my only hope," I said, looking down at my feet. Howard noticed the sneakers for the first time. "Ahhh, Bent. Those are . . . ummmm . . ."

"UGGGLLLY," I said. "But we're going to change them. Let me have the paint."

Howard handed me the can. "How will it make them better?"

"Ever seen camouflage sneakers?" I leaned over and started to spray.

"Maybe you ought to take them off first, Bent. You're spraying your socks," Howard pointed out.

I kicked off the sneakers. The blotches I was spraying would look like camouflage . . . I hoped. "Well? What do you think? Better?"

Howard shrugged. "Interesting."

"Okay," I stepped back for a better look. Then I squinted at the sneakers and walked around to look at them from the other side. "I don't know, Howie. They sure smell." I sat down to brush the leaves off my socks and put my sneakers on.

"They're sticky, too," I said, wiping a smeared finger on the grass.

"We'd better hurry. We'll miss the bus," Howard warned. "I hear it over on the next block."

"Do you think people are born cool, or get to be cool?" I asked as we bounced along on the bus a few minutes later.

Howard shrugged. "Don't know. Why?"

"Oh, no reason, except I thought this ought to be the year. We can't wait too long. I think being cool will take some practice if you aren't born that way . . . and there's a chance we weren't."

"Nine out of ten child psychologists say that kids our age become obsessed with being cool," Howard said.

"And four out of five fifth graders don't know what 'obsessed' means," I admitted.

Howard pulled his dictionary from his book bag. " 'Obsessed — preoccupied with, having a one-track mind, fixated.' "

"Oh." I thought that four out of five fifth graders wouldn't be too sure about "preoccupied" and "fixated," either, but I decided to drop it.

A few minutes later, I said, "I've ditched my lunch box. I bag it now."

"Yeah? Why?" Howard asked.

"Cooler."

Howard nodded. "The in-word for the year is definitely 'cool.' "

34

*   *   *

The bus jounced into the school yard and stopped in front of the building. I glanced out the window and saw big Anthony Magliari strutting by the bus, heading toward a group of Colleen's friends.

I jabbed Howard in the side with my elbow. "There. You see?" I pointed toward Anthony. "That guy is living, breathing, coolness. Look at him." I wondered if I'd ever be big and awesome instead of scrawny and average.

"Definitely born-that-way cool, not to mention tough," Howard said as we watched Anthony approach the crowd of girls. "But, don't forget, he's way older than we are."

"You're not kidding."

Anthony Magliari was practically a man. I think he probably shaved. For the past couple of summers Anthony had worked with his father's construction company. He was no regular kid.

I clomped off the bus in my too-big, camouflage, frog sneakers. My chances of looking cool that day were zero, lunch bag or no lunch bag. If people said, "WOW!" it wouldn't be for the right reason.

The bell to let us in the building hadn't rung yet. I looked down at my frog feet. On the grass they'd show less than on the blacktop. I hopped onto the grass, into the tallest patch I could find.

"Hi, Bently," a voice said behind me.

As I turned and saw Lisa, my face got hot. I

hoped my ears weren't glowing at the same time.

What would Lisa Rogers, the prettiest girl in the world, do when she realized that she was standing next to the boy with the doofiest sneakers in the world? Run? Scream?

"What are you doing?" she asked.

"Ummm, looking for a quarter I dropped," I said, quickly squatting, hoping to hide the sneakers. I pretended to look through the grass.

The bell rang. I took a deep breath and stood up.

Lisa didn't say anything . . . not even about the dirt, grass, and leaves stuck to my sneakers. As we walked toward the building, I tried to scuff my sneakers together to clean them off. It wasn't easy walking that way, and I was sure she must be thinking how weird my sneakers and I were.

She's being polite, I thought. She'd like to get away from me, but she's too nice. I wished she'd just say something and get it over with.

We reached the door, and Lisa did say something. She said, "Bently, those sneakers are great. Where'd you get them? I love them!"

"I-I-I'm not . . . ummm, well, they . . ." I fumbled with my answer. "Oh, in some mall."

"They're cool," she said.

What? Really? No kidding? Wow.

I began to strut a bit as I walked. Cool guys do that.

7.
Octopus Duty

Mr. Corby was poking through the clutter on his desk as we walked into the classroom. A large brown stain was on the front of his shirt. Coffee, for sure.

I opened my desk and tossed in a bunch of colored pencils from home. Then I looked over at Lisa. She was talking to her friend Kathryn while she took some erasers, pencils, and pens from a bag and put them on her desk.

"My father got me these. He said they'd help start the year off," Lisa explained. In the right corner of her desk she placed two fancy rainbow erasers on either side of her new pencils. The pencils had tiny chains coming out of the tops with little stars dangling from them. Next, she held up some pens, the kind that smell like different fruits. "Want one?" she said to Kathryn. "Take your pick."

I guess not all girls were like my sister. Lisa shared without being forced or threatened.

"Thanks!" Kathryn said, choosing a cherry-red pen. I heard Kathryn call across to Maria and ask her what her favorite song was. The girls talked about rock singers. I thought about what I'd say if they asked me. The song I really liked best was a commercial for an airline.

Patty was standing by Maureen's desk. I wondered if she actually liked Maureen, or was afraid of her. Maybe since Maureen was nasty mostly to boys, girls didn't mind her. Besides, her mother worked at McDonald's, and Maureen was always handing out McDonald's cookies to the girls.

Patty giggled as Maureen said loudly, "Boys are alien life forms."

I pulled my feet as far under my desk as possible, figuring that Lisa might be the only fifth grader to like my sneakers. Maureen's next line might be: "Boys are alien life forms wearing disgusting-looking, nerdy sneakers." I decided I better hide my feet altogether. So I sat on them.

Then a terrible thought came over me. If the paint on my sneakers wasn't dry, the seat of my pants could look awful. I could have the imprint of two feet on my rear end. I might have to stay in that chair for the rest of my life.

"Pssst, Howie," I whispered quietly.

Howard didn't hear me. He just scratched his ear and kept reading.

I took out some paper and wrote:

> Howard — Don't say anything.
> Check my pants. Any paint?

I folded it, then stopped and unfolded it. I added:

> P.S. Or any grass or leaves stuck
> on?

I leaned behind Peggy and tossed the note to Howard. Then I eased up off my feet again and waited for Howard to look. He scowled at the note, then looked my way. He took a pencil from his desk and wrote on the back of my note:

> Not much paint. Just the shape of
> two heels... and a little grass. Just
> brush off.

I swallowed hard. JUST two heels! JUST brush off! Oh, yeah, easy for Howard to say. *His* hind end didn't look as if it had been kicked by a mule.

I put my feet down and wondered how I was going to get through the day without everyone laughing themselves crazy over my pants. I sure picked the wrong day to think about becoming cool.

Mr. Corby cleared his throat and said to the class, "I'm assigning some classroom jobs for this week. Willie — you'll be our message carrier.

Maria, you'll be the door holder. Bently, you'll feed Archie."

I gulped. Mr. Corby went on giving out jobs, but I stopped listening. This day just kept getting worse.

I pictured myself standing by the tank, dropping in food. Suddenly a long, sucker-covered arm flashed out of the water, wrapped itself around my neck, and yanked me in. I was gone with barely a trace . . . just a few bubbles . . . and one green sneaker floating on top of the water.

"Devilfish is another name for octopus," Howard whispered, holding up a book on sea life.

"That figures," I muttered.

"Oh, wow, get this — it has that nickname because of its fierce-looking, glaring eyes and its long coiling arms," Howard said. "The common octopi grow to about ten feet, and the giant ones can be over thirty feet," he said.

"Oh, great. How big *is* that guy, anyway? He looks like Moby Dick."

"Moby Dick was a whale, dummy. And Archie isn't very big."

"Yet," I added. "What do octopi eat, anyway?"

"Oh, fish, prawns, crabs, and stuff like that," Howard said.

I looked around the room. No fish or prawns. No crabs, either . . . unless crabby Maureen counted. What was I supposed to feed that octopus?

Mr. Corby must have been reading my mind. "All right. We need to get settled. Most of the classroom jobs I've assigned are familiar. But the animal feeders will need to see me after lunch. I'll explain your jobs." Mr. Corby unscrewed his thermos and poured coffee into his plastic cup.

For a while I forgot to worry about my pants and worried about my job. My luck wasn't very good with things that live in water. Last year I'd let Ruckles out of his turtle bowl to walk around my bedroom. Then I had gone downstairs for a snack and heard my mom yell. I ran upstairs and there was Ruckles, sucked to the end of the vacuum hose. He was dazed, but unhurt.

Back in July, when Howard was going to the shore for a week, he asked me to take care of his goldfish, Alice.

"What if something happens to her?" I had asked.

"Don't worry, she hasn't died in all these months," Howard had answered. "She's not going to do it now."

Howard had been wrong. The morning after he left, Alice was belly up. I shook the bowl and yelled at her. "Get up, Alice! Get up! If this is some sick trick Howard taught you, just to scare me, cut it out!" I'd even dropped an aspirin tablet in. Nothing. In the end, I froze Alice until Howard got home, so he could bury her the way he wanted.

A week later, we placed a very stiff and cold

41

Alice in a sardine can. We said a few solemn words, and buried her among the geraniums near Howard's mailbox.

What if Archie died, as Alice had? Maybe I should warn Mr. Corby about my unlucky past. I opened my desk and took out my goal book.

MY GOALS - PARTS THREE AND FOUR

I don't want to turn into Bloody Bently the Octopus Murderer
and
I don't ever want to get out of my chair.

8.
Slime Ball

For once, I was glad to be in the middle groups. I didn't have to move for reading and math. And even though I wanted to go to the bathroom and get a drink, I stayed put and kept my rear end out of sight.

I did have to get up for lunch, though. But I waited until everyone else was in line before I stood. No way did I want anyone behind my behind.

Holding my lunch in back of me, hoping it would block the heel marks, I followed Howard into the lunchroom. "Why is it that even after this place has a whole summer to air out, it still has the same smell?" I asked, looking for a place to sit down fast.

Howard shrugged. He was watching the hot dogs float in greasy water next to a tub of sauerkraut.

"And why is it that it always smells like *this* lunch, even when it isn't this lunch?" I went on.

"Don't know. You're lucky, though," Howard said. "You brought yours. No way am I going to buy one of those waterlogged hot dogs. When you bite them, they squirt stuff that looks like duck pee."

"Oh, jeez, Howie. Enough." I headed toward a table, wanting my seat in a seat as soon as possible.

Howard looked around. "Maybe I can make a deal with someone. Be right back." He headed for the tables of fourth graders who shared the same lunch period.

I sat down next to Louie and across from Andy and Willie. Andy leaned down and looked at my sneakers. If he thought they were weird, he ought to see my pants.

Howard went from person to person, seeing what they brought and trying to trade his lunch money. Finally I heard him say, "Awww right!" Grinning, he hurried back to the table carrying a paper sack that read SALLY'S BAG. I wondered about Sally. She couldn't know she just traded a good lunch for something filled with duck pee.

"Whatcha got?" I asked, wondering if maybe this wheeling and dealing thing could have possibilities . . . especially since I'd just opened up my own sandwich, and noticed the tomato slice had sogged up the bread, and the lettuce seemed to have slid into one half of the sandwich, collapsed, and died.

44

"Hmmm, let's look," Howard said, pulling out a carton of chocolate milk, followed by a bag of chips. "So far, not bad." A peanut butter-and-jelly sandwich on squishy white bread (the kind neither of our mothers would buy) was next. "Oh, yes," he said, smiling. Last, out came one of those little crackers-and-cheese packages — the kind with a little square cup of cheese, and a little piece of plastic to try to spread it with.

"Luucckky," I said, just as a cheese puff sailed past my ear. Andy grinned, and Willie whistled innocently. "Oh, yeah?" I flicked a grape across the table.

"War!" shouted Willie, flicking three more cheese puffs my way, hitting Louie.

"Oh, NO, you don't!" Cannonball, the lunch aide, loomed over us, glaring. Her shape explained her name. "There will be *NO* food fights!" From below, I looked up her hairy, red nostrils, which puffed angrily.

"Okay," Louie said, nodding seriously.

"This whole table will stay inside to clean up when the others are dismissed." She scowled at us. "Winning 'Best Lunch Bunch' means nothing to you, huh?" She turned and stalked away.

"Oh, great," muttered Andy. "Now we're stuck sweeping garbage when we could be outside stuffing leaves down people's shirts. This stinks."

"Yeah," said Willie. He squirted catsup on his

potato chips. "Hmmm. Not bad," he said between crunches.

"Let me try," said Andy.

"You'll get sick," Louie warned.

"Hold it. The catsup's plugged," Willie said, fiddling with the top. "Okay, here ya go."

He grinned as he watched Andy begin to squirt.

"AHHHH!" yelled Andy as the top flew off and catsup gushed all over his plate. "You dork! You *loosened* it!" Andy threw his napkin at Willie. Willie ducked and kept grinning.

Cannonball glared at them from across the cafeteria. They quieted down.

Lunch over, I looked at the floor and nearly gagged. Kids had dropped, spilled, and mashed every kind of food there was. Trying to hide my pants, I stayed close to the floor.

When I came to the most revolting part of the floor, I knew it was where Harry Leonard had sat. Lunchmixer Leonard. There were mashed remains of parts of lots of lunches mixed together. That was what Harry did. When people dared him to eat terrible mixtures, he did. At recess he usually had a sick expression on his face. Once he even threw up. Then he got another nickname — Harry the Heaver.

Cannonball came over to inspect our work. "Not too bad. Next time you'll think twice before you throw food." She looked at us without smiling.

I wouldn't argue with Cannonball if I was paid a bundle to. Last spring she slid, lost her balance, and landed on Frank Tantini. He was squashed practically flat. There was no way I wanted to end up like Flat Frank.

Cannonball finally let us go, but by the time we got to the playground, it was time to go in. I went to the back of the line and kept my rear to the building.

"Shoot me if I get stuck at a food fight table with a bunch of bums again," Howard said.

"Ha!" I punched his arm. "I saw you flick that chip."

"Not me. I know better," Howard said, pushing up his glasses and grinning.

"Slime ball," I said.

"Who is?" Maureen asked loudly, two inches from my ear.

I ignored her.

"*Who* is!" She repeated. "*WHO?*"

"None of your business," I said.

"Yeah, well, it couldn't be anyone important. You'd be too much of a wuss to call anyone who's a big shot 'slime ball.' "

I was about to call nosy Maureen "the biggest slime ball of all time" when I remembered the time she bit right through Andy's winter jacket and he had to go get a shot — probably a rabies shot.

Not wanting Maureen to think I was scared of

her, or anyone else, I said, "Anthony Magliari." There. She got her answer. Yup, she sure did. And what an answer.

"Oooh, I'm telling!" she squealed. "Hey! Bently called Anthony Magliari a slime ball!"

That got everyone excited. The line turned and looked at me. "Ooooh," exclaimed about five girls at once. I knew instantly how totally uncool, along with stupid, I was.

"You're gonna get it, Bently Barker. You're gonna get creamed," Maureen said. She tossed her head back and put her hands on her hips.

"Nice move, Bent. You just insulted the school's toughest kid," said Howard.

"Oohh, m'gosh," Louie exclaimed, shaking his head. "Oohh, oohh, oohh . . . m'gosh."

I began to sweat. I mopped my forehead with my arm. The story of the boy David and the giant Goliath popped into my head. What a way to make a name for myself.

9.
Meeting Danger
Head-on

" **A**ll right," Mr. Corby said when we were back in the classroom. "I need to talk with my animal feeders."

I stared at Mr. Corby's tongue. It was black. I hoped it had gotten that way from sucking on licorice. Otherwise, it was pretty creepy.

Mr. Corby made feeding Archie sound simple. All I had to do was take one of the little bags of frozen prawns from the small refrigerator in the teachers' room, and drop prawns into the aquarium.

Backside to the wall, I walked down the hall toward the teachers' room. I knocked on the door and explained to Mrs. McDougall, Colleen's seventh-grade teacher, that I was there for octopus food. Mrs. McDougall gave me a weird look and pointed to the refrigerator. "We'd better speak to Warren about what he's putting next to our lunches," she said to another teacher.

I walked silently to the refrigerator. I couldn't wait to get out of that room.

As I walked out the door, I crashed into the bottom two thirds of Anthony Magliari. Anthony's top third was over my head.

My knees wobbled as I backed up. Anthony smirked. "Watch where you're going," he said, standing in the doorway and dabbing a wet paper towel on his knuckles.

"Not again, Anthony." Mrs. McDougall sighed. "Another fight?"

Anthony nodded and mumbled something that sounded like, "No one bothers my girl."

Walking quickly back to my classroom, I wondered who Anthony's girl was. At least she had one thing going for her — Anthony was fighting for her, not against her.

Holding the bag behind me, I carried the stinky octopus food to Archie's tank. Cautiously, I peered in. Archie didn't lunge at me, squirt ink, or even move. "Come and get it, Archie." I saw Archie behind his rock. "Hey, Arch. Chow time."

I dropped in some smelly food, but Archie didn't budge. Oh, please, Archie, don't be sick . . . or dead. Maybe Archie wasn't hungry. Maybe he'd been punched out by Anthony Magliari for touching his girlfriend.

I dropped in more food. Archie began to wave one tentacle slowly. Phew, he lives.

"Bently, are you nearly done? We need to start social studies," Mr. Corby said.

I emptied the rest of the bag into the water as I watched the octopus move toward the food. Archie was creepy, but he didn't look like a man-eating sea monster. "Well, Archie," I said, "I guess you're not going to attack me after all. Let's hope Anthony Magliari feels the same way."

Howard calmly walked by and handed me a note.

Maureen says she's personally going to tell Anthony that you called him a slime ball.

I looked down at my green feet. Maybe I should have camouflaged my whole body.

10.
Stalked by Anthony Magliari

Anthony Magliari stomped all over my sleep that night. With every toss and turn, I found myself face to face with a snarling Anthony . . . an Anthony that stood as tall, and weighed as much, as a bus.

I felt tired when I woke up. I wondered if Anthony had spent his night plotting revenge. Probably not. Big guys don't have to plot . . . they just flatten.

Maybe Anthony wouldn't be in school. He probably would. Tough guys don't get sick. Maybe Anthony would skip school.

I knew I should have tried right away to talk Maureen out of tattling, but I just couldn't force myself to beg. Maybe she hadn't said anything yet. Maybe she could be bribed. Food? Or maybe Colleen had something Maureen would like.

I lay in bed worrying and listening to the morning noises in my house.

"You're going to be late, Bent. Up and at 'em," called my dad from the foot of the stairs.

Being late used to seem like a terrible thing. I'd always figured that people who were late had to go to the principal's office to be yelled at, and that was scary. But now that didn't seem so terrible, at least not compared to being smushed into the ground.

I groaned and flung my leg over the side of my bed. There was a surprised dog yelp from below as Farful scrambled out of the way.

"Sorry, Farful." I reached under the bed and patted her head.

"What's going on?" Mom called down the hall.

"It's okay. I stepped on Farful," I answered.

"Klutz," Colleen commented on her way to the bathroom.

What a crummy day it was already. And I hadn't even faced Anthony yet.

Colleen was singing "Twist and Shout" in the bathroom.

I howled like a hound dog, then started down the hall toward Colleen's room. There had to be something in there that I could use to bribe Maureen. I reached for a bracelet I'd given Colleen but had never seen her wear. Suddenly I heard whistling outside.

I stood for a second, hand outstretched. Then I glanced out the window and froze. There, leaning against a tree in front of my house, was Anthony Magliari. My stomach turned to ice. My head began to throb. I ducked down and crawled away from the window.

What now? How long could I stay in the house? Till I grew bigger than Anthony? That might be never. Could I tell my parents I needed protection? That was wimpy. Maybe I could get a gang together, a gang of bodyguards. But who'd want the job of protecting my body against the world's biggest seventh grader? Their own bodies must mean something to them.

I crawled out of the bedroom.

At breakfast I poked at my pancakes until they were a gooey, syrupy mush. Anthony Magliari had probably eaten the breakfast of champions — raw meat with nails on top — and was doing push-ups outside. I opened a jar of peanut butter and plopped a glob on my pancakes.

"Mom, Bently's being disgusting again," Colleen reported.

"What are you doing?" Mom asked me.

"Trying to get strong — fast," I mumbled. "I might not live through this day, you know."

I waited to hear my family tell me how much I meant to them and how worried they were. But instead, Mom said, "Bently, I put the pants you wore yesterday into the washer and noticed some stains. Did you sit on something?"

I nodded. If she thinks those paint stains are

something, wait'll she sees the blood stains that are next.

"What kind of sandwich do you want today, Bent — peanut butter?" Dad asked, opening a loaf of bread.

"Guess so," I answered. "But I might not have any teeth left in my mouth by lunchtime." Nobody paid any attention. I felt like screaming, "Doesn't anyone *realize* that this might be the end for me?"

"Our class is having a talent show in November," Colleen said. "I'm going to sing."

"What song — 'You ain't nothin' but a hound dog'?" I mumbled.

"Talent shows can be fun," Mom said, pouring her tea.

"They're supposed to be," Colleen answered, "but *some* jealous people, such as Danielle and dopey Buford, spoil things."

"What did Danielle and Buford do?"

On my way out of the kitchen, I stopped to hear what Danielle and Buford had done. It might be interesting.

"Nasty remarks. They said I sing through my nose."

It wasn't interesting, it was just true. If an anteater could sing, it would sound like Colleen.

When I reached the door to my bedroom, I got down and crawled to the window. Slowly, I straightened up until my nose was on the windowsill and my eyes just at tree level. As

I stood up more, I let out a sigh. No Anthony Magliari.

What if he were hiding . . . waiting. Behind a tree? Around the corner?

I usually walked to the bus stop alone, but this morning I stalled while Colleen got ready. She was fixing her hair. "You know that bracelet I gave you for your last birthday?" I tried to sound casual so maybe she'd give me the bracelet without thinking much about it.

"Hmmm. You mean the sparkly bangle one?"

"Yeah. You didn't like it too much, did you?"

Colleen paused for a moment. "Why?"

Uh-oh. She was thinking about it. "Umm. I kind of need a present for a girl," I said.

Colleen spun around in her chair. "Oooh, Bently, you have a girlfriend." She grinned at me in a really annoying way. I should have just taken the dumb bracelet when she wasn't looking.

I gritted my teeth. The only thing worse than having Anthony Magliari slaughter me would be having Maureen as a girlfriend . . . and Colleen knowing about it.

"Well, all right. You can have it, even if it *is* one of my favorite things." She grinned. "Since it's for a good cause."

Five minutes later, Colleen and I called good-bye and started out the door. I hung back on the porch steps as I looked for Anthony. The coast seemed clear, and the bus was just coming around the corner.

"Come on, slowpoke! Race you!" I scrambled down the steps and tore past Colleen.

We dashed toward the bus. I raced faster than I'd ever run. I got to the bus first and thumped on the door for the driver to open up.

"Come on, come on," I whispered, panting.

Climbing up into the bus, I looked back over my shoulder. Down the street . . . sitting on his dirt bike . . . staring straight at us . . . was Anthony Magliari.

11.
Blackmail

"You don't look so hot," Howard said as I sagged into the bus seat, breathing hard.

"Check outside," I answered, pointing in the direction of Anthony Magliari.

"Aaaah. No wonder," he said. "Well, maybe Anthony has a morning paper route."

"Nope. A truck delivers them."

The bus pulled away and drove down the street. I looked out the window to see if Anthony was following.

"See him?" Howard asked.

"No. But he's out there somewhere." I stared at the seat in front of me. After a moment I said, "I wonder how many weeks I could hide out on this bus."

"I'd say that eight out of ten people who try to hide on buses get caught," Howard said.

"Thanks for sharing that. What if Anthony's waiting at school when the bus pulls in? I bet he's pedaling like crazy to beat us there," I said. The image of the Headless Horseman thundering after Ichabod Crane flashed through my mind.

The bus groaned to a stop, and the doors rattle-thwacked open.

I took several long, deep breaths and tried to prepare my brain for what was ahead. It was in charge of my body, and I wanted it ready. I began to hum the song from the movie *Rocky*.

Howard stared at my frog sneakers and quietly suggested, "Maybe you ought to hum 'It's not easy being green.' "

The bus driver turned around in his seat, raised one eyebrow, and said, "Well? You getting out?"

"You better tie your sneaker lace," Howard advised.

"Nah," I answered. "All the older kids wear them like this." I stopped to look left and right before stepping down from the bus . . . just in case. As I started out the door, one of my untied, too-big, green sneakers dropped off and bounced to the pavement ahead of me. I was pretty sure I heard snickering. Muttering to myself, "Way to go, klutz. Nice entrance," I hopped off the bus and angrily jammed my foot into the sneaker.

A group of fifth-grade girls stood watching on the blacktop. Lisa was one of them. I glanced her way before striding toward the playing field.

"Where are you going, Bent?" Howard asked, running after me.

I kept going, with Howard beside me. I wasn't

sure where I was walking, but I knew that a moving target was harder to hit.

I heard someone behind us. I walked faster. So did the footsteps.

"Hey!" a voice called out.

I caught my breath and turned. It was Maureen.

"G'morning Bently." She jammed her hands into her pants pockets and smiled.

She had a weird smile — big grinny teeth, but scowly eyebrows. I waited for her to say something else.

"I'll bet you want to know what I told Anthony."

I did, and I didn't.

Howard stepped forward and looked up at her. "Look, Maureen, don't you know tattling stinks? And nine out of ten tattlers get warts." He moved back out of range, just in case.

"Well . . ." she drew it out suspensefully, "maybe . . ." she went on in a teasing tone.

"Maybe what?" I asked.

"Just maybe . . ." She smiled at me. "Just maybe I didn't tell *yet* and maybe I could be persuaded not to."

"Blackmail," Howard whispered.

"Hold it . . . wait," I said, confused. "You mean you *didn't* tell?" I dug down into my pants pocket and pulled up Colleen's bracelet. "Want this?" I asked, holding it out.

Maureen leaned toward the bracelet, then made

a face. "No, I don't like plastic jewelry. But . . . if you have a party and invite me . . ." I stood there with my mouth open. An image flashed through my head of Maureen marching around my house, giving orders to everyone. I groaned.

Howard took off his glasses and wiped them on his shirt as he waited for me to say something.

I dug the toe of my sneaker into the dirt. "Uh — mmm. I wasn't going to have a party, that I know of."

"Make one." She stared at me without blinking.

I looked back into her eyes. Then something clicked. Maureen must be lying. "Hey, you must have told already. Anthony Magliari was hanging around my house this morning."

Maureen looked confused for a moment. "He was? Oh." She pushed some hair behind her ear. "Well, maybe I did . . . and maybe I didn't. I see him all the time. He only lives two streets away from me, and I know his sister personally."

Howard was thinking out loud. "Hmmm . . . but if you didn't tell, who did? Or maybe he was just out walking his dog."

"Anthony doesn't have a dog," Maureen said.

The bell rang, and kids began to file inside the building. We started back across the field toward school.

"Well?" said Maureen. "What's it going to be?"

"I have to think," I said. I'd never been stalked and blackmailed all in one morning.

Howard elbowed me and whispered, "I don't trust her."

"I heard you," Maureen hissed.

As we walked toward the building, my untied sneakers slapped the ground. Maureen looked down at my feet, back to me, then at my feet again. "Never saw sneakers like those." She made a face.

"They're custom designed — *very* hard to get," Howard said.

Maureen looked at him doubtfully. "Really?"

Howard nodded seriously.

Maureen took a second look, but said nothing.

Howard nudged me and grinned.

We got to the door. Just as Howard reached out to hold it open, he murmured, "Uh-oh."

I looked where he was staring. Inside stood Anthony Magliari.

The line of kids was pressing from behind, pushing me forward. I tried not to look at Anthony, but I couldn't help it. I wanted to be ready to duck, dodge, run — maybe all three at once. But Anthony just watched me. It seemed as if he wanted to say something, something I was sure I wouldn't want to hear. Maybe Anthony was the kind of guy who terrorizes people in private. It might be a good idea to hang out with a crowd.

The flow of kids moved me along. Howard sighed loudly as we neared our classroom door. "Close call, Bent."

Maureen grabbed my sleeve before I went into the room. "Tell me by twelve o'clock what you're going to do, Bently." She leaned against the door frame. Then she jabbed me in the chest with her finger. "Twelve o'clock."

12.
Forgotten

*B*AM! A note from Maureen landed like a rock on my desk at nine-thirty.

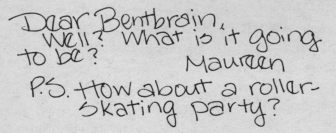

Dear Bentbrain,
   Well? What is it going to be?
            Maureen
P.S. How about a roller-skating party?

BAM! A second note hit at ten o'clock.

Bentman,
   Or a pizza party.
            Maureen

As if the messages from Maureen weren't bad enough, at ten-fifteen I saw Anthony Magliari walk past the door and peer in. Everything in my body turned to ice. I shut my eyes . . . and when

I opened them, Anthony was gone. Maybe I'd imagined him.

Mr. Corby's coffee breath and the words "Having trouble, Bently?" startled me. He was leaning over my shoulder, looking at my paper. His tongue was licorice-black again.

Trouble? What a question. Boy, would Warren ever be surprised if I told him just how much trouble I was having. "Uh, I don't know. Maybe I'm sick or something."

"I think it would be a good idea for the nurse to check you, Bently." He glanced quickly around the room, then added, "Louie? You certainly know the way to the nurse's office. Go with Bently, then come back." Already Louie held the record for the most trips to the nurse.

Mr. Corby patted me on the shoulder. "Don't worry, Bently. The nurse will probably send you back soon, which is good because we're going to be talking about our goals later."

Coming back in one piece is a good goal, I thought. But not likely with little Louie, the tiniest kid in the class, as my bodyguard. Anthony'd love this.

"Why are you walking like that?" Louie asked, looking at me curiously.

"Like how?"

"Like this." Louie took two steps, stopped, and looked right. Then he took two more steps, stopped, and looked left. "Huh? Why are you walking weird? What's the matter with you?"

"Uh, well . . . I . . ." I fumbled, ". . . nerve problem." I felt sure that any moment Anthony would come springing out from a doorway or from around a corner. "I don't have long to live."

Louie backed up a few steps. Then there was silence as Louie thought. He stood with his hand on his forehead and mumbled, "Oohh, my gosh. I've never taken anyone to the nurse who might not ever come back." He looked at his watch. "I'd better not wait for you, then."

Five minutes later I was resting on a cot behind a curtain. Mrs. Von Dorf, the nurse, had told me I had no fever. That figured — even my temperature was average.

Mrs. Von Dorf suggested that I lie down for a while. Somewhere between listening to Mrs. Von Dorf telephone a parent about someone's throat culture, and hearing a teacher ask for two aspirins, I went to sleep.

"Well, my goodness gracious," Mrs. Von Dorf exclaimed. "How ever could I have forgotten you were here!" She was bending over me, nudging my arm. "I had so many phone calls and interruptions, and you were so quiet. . . ." She shook her head. "It's nearly lunchtime, Bently."

I stared at her and blinked a few times. That

proved it. I was definitely average, so average I'd been forgotten.

"Do you feel better after your rest?"

"I guess so."

"Fine, then you may return to class," Mrs. Von Dorf said.

I stood up, checked the hall, and headed back to my homeroom. The class was probably discussing goals.

Goalwise, things sure weren't going so well. At least not for my number-one goal. It was going nowhere. Too bad my pen couldn't just suck up the ink off the page where I'd written that goal so I could start over. I should have been more definite about what I wanted. I wanted to *stand* out, not *lie* out flat on the ground, with Anthony Magliari towering above me, resting his big foot on my chest, and Maureen Hiffard cackling from the sidelines.

MY GOAL— PART FIVE

I want to make a name for myself ... and then stay alive to enjoy it.

13.
What's Going On?

I walked to my desk to get my lunch. The room was so quiet that I could hear only the sound of my untied sneakers slapping the floor. I began picking my feet up high, as if I were wading through a swamp.

Andy poked Willie in the shoulder when Willie started to speak, and Lisa stood by her desk staring at me. She looked as if she were about to cry.

The classroom door opened, and Howard walked in. "Howard," Mr. Corby said, "any trouble finding Mr. Lewis? I forgot to tell you he's in a different classroom this year." Mr. Lewis was a special teacher who worked with kids who were extra smart. Howard was in his class a few hours a week.

Howard shook his head. "No problem." He dropped his books on his desk. "Oops, sorry," he said when he realized how quiet the room had been. "What's going on?" he whispered to Louie, who didn't answer.

BAM! I didn't even have to look down to know that another note from Maureen had landed on my desk. The bell for lunch rang, and while kids lined up at the door, I unfolded the note.

Dear Bently,
    Forget about Anthony and everthing. I didn't Know.
                    Maureen

What did that mean? I looked up, just as Kathryn patted me gently on the shoulder on her way to the door. "Here, for you," Lisa said, laying a grape-flavored pen on my desk.

The bell rang, and Mr. Corby led the line from the room. Only Howard and I were left. I picked up the grape pen and sniffed it.

"Did the class get in trouble or what? And why'd Lisa give you that pen?" Howard asked.

"Don't know. I just got back from the nurse. Everyone's acting weird." I held out Maureen's note. "Look at this."

Howard scratched his head. "Wonder what she means, 'I didn't know' — know what? How to spell? She's a rotten speller."

"I have no idea what she meant." I crumpled the note and tossed it into the garbage. "That girl's strange."

Howard and I walked into the lunchroom a few minutes later. Heads turned and eyes stared. "This is creepy," Howard whispered as we headed for the table where Andy and Willie were sitting. "Why's everyone looking at us?"

I shrugged.

"I'll be back. I've got to hurry and see what I can trade for my lunch money," Howard said, heading for a table of girls.

I sat across from Willie. "Hi. What's up?"

Willie shook his head. "Nothin'."

Andy agreed. "Nothin'." Then he pushed his bag of Cheez Doodles toward me. "Here. You can have these."

"And this," Willie added, sliding his chocolate cupcake my way.

"You guys sick or something?" I asked. Neither of them had ever given me the favorite parts of their lunches before.

"Sick? Us? Ahhh, no," Andy answered. "How are *you*?"

"Better," I answered.

"That's good," Andy and Willie said together.

Howard slid on to the bench next to me and dumped an armload of food — three Twinkies, two Devil Dogs, two bags of chips . . . "Jeez, Howie. You're a master at this lunch-dealing business," I said.

"A lot of this is for you," Howard explained,

just as Cannonball, the lunch aide, peered over his shoulder at the pile of sweets.

"Me? Why? I've got lunch," I said.

"Beats me," Howard said. "All I know is that people kept handing me stuff and saying it was for you."

"Want some?" I offered the others.

"Sure," Howard answered, grinning broadly. "What a haul." Then he flinched and looked under the table. "Hey, you, Bozo, why'd you kick me?" he asked Willie.

Willie glared at him. Howard stared back, confused. He looked at me, but I was no help. "Okay, someone tell us what's going on!" Howard said.

We waited. No one spoke. We looked at Andy, at Willie, and at the kids down at the end of the table across from Louie. Silence.

It seemed as if the whole fifth-grade side of the lunchroom suddenly got quiet. I felt my face getting red, then my ears. Howard looked around, and finally said, "*All right! What* is it!? Come on!"

Silence. Then, slowly, kids began getting up, throwing out their trash, and going outside. On their way past me, Audrey and Maria each set down a cookie. "Thanks," I said as I picked one up and took a bite. Between chews I mumbled, "Whatever's going on, at least we're eating well."

"Yeah, but this is starting to feel like a science fiction movie," Howard commented.

I nodded. "I think it began with my green Martian sneakers. Or maybe that alien octopus, or maybe Warren himself is an extraterrestrial, and he's captured Mrs. Evans, who didn't move at all. Maybe she's in prison on another planet, or she was turned into Jughead the iguana." I was really getting into it. "And what about that black tongue of his? What do you think?"

"Ten out of ten people who eat black licorice get black tongues. And those Twinkies have gone to your brain." Howard snatched one from my hand. "Let's go."

Cannonball nodded at us as we tossed the armload of sweets into the trash. But on the way out, I glanced back over my shoulder. I saw Cannonball reach into the can and pull out a cupcake.

I was still trying to figure out what was going on as we walked back to class. As far as I could tell, kids were feeling sorry for me, but I didn't have a clue why.

"They can't be feeling bad that Anthony Magliari's going to get me," I said to Howard.

"Nope," Howard agreed. "And the way Maureen's big mouth works, they'd all know she'd changed her mind about tattling."

Maybe if they saw that I was cool and in control, they'd relax and act normal. When it was time to feed Archie, I whistled and bopped as I walked past Lisa, swinging the bag of octopus food. Then I turned my back to the tank and flipped a prawn over my shoulder into the water. Pretty slick move.

Howard laughed, but that was it. Everyone else just stared.

"Bently," Mr. Corby said, "a little less flourish. Just drop the food in. We've got something important to talk about."

14.
Warren's Goal

"All right kids, I'm going to give you ten minutes to think about your goals," Mr. Corby said. "Put them on paper, if you haven't already done so."

I stared at my goals — parts one, two, three, four, and five. I had a feeling that Mr. Corby hadn't meant for the whole business to get so involved. I turned to a fresh page in my goal book and wrote out my first goal again.

I want to be outstanding, not
boring. When other Kids think
of me, I want them to go, "Wow!"

That's enough. I shouldn't have to explain that I don't mean for people to go, "Wow! There goes the kid in the painted sneakers!" or, "Wow! There goes the kid Anthony Magliari is after." I want kids to say, "Wow! There goes Bently Barker. That boy is really something!"

I stared at my paper, then glanced around the room. I looked at Lisa. What kind of goal could she have — where do you go from perfect?

Mr. Corby took a sip of leftover lunch coffee from his plastic cup, licked his lips, and said, "All right, gang. Let's talk for a few minutes."

Louie's hand shot up. "The goal can be short, can't it?"

Short kid, short goal, I thought.

"Okay, class, I promised you that you could keep your goals private," Mr. Corby said. "I also said that you could hand in your goal books and share your goals with me. Eventually, maybe later in the year, some of you may even want to talk about your goal with the rest of us."

Mr. Corby looked out over his silent class. "Anyone want to share a goal with me?"

We all looked back at him and around at each other.

He tossed up a piece of chalk and caught it. "Anyone? If you'd like to hand in your goal books now, I'll take them home over the weekend, and get them back to you Monday."

Again, kids looked around at each other. Then Audrey held her book up toward Mr. Corby. Maria, Howard, Kathryn, and Louie did the same. That was it. The rest kept theirs.

I was wondering if I'd ever hand in my goal book when Mr. Corby said, "Now, I'm going to share one of my goals with you. It involves you." He pointed to the class.

That's a tricky way to give us another goal, Warren, I thought.

"I think students in the different grades of a school should get to know one another and work together," Mr. Corby said. "One of my goals is to make that happen."

Here goes — Warren's going to tell us to all bring shovels or hammers or brushes tomorrow. We're going to build a science lab or paint the gym.

"Most of you, I'm sure, can remember back to when you were in the lower grades," Mr. Corby continued. "You looked up to the older students and thought they were grown up and important."

Some of them *still* look pretty grown up to me. Anthony, for one.

Kids nodded and began telling memories of when they were younger. "I even remember begging my kindergarten teacher for *homework*," admitted Kathryn.

"Me, too," Lisa added. "I wanted it so I could complain about it like the big kids did."

"All right, now," Mr. Corby said. "Here's what I want to try. I'd like to match each of you up with a younger child in the school. You'd be like big buddies. I've spoken to lower-grade teachers, and we're working on a list of younger kids who could use your help. We won't start right away, but in a few weeks. What do you think?"

"What kind of help?" Peggy and Patty asked at the same time.

"All kinds," Mr. Corby answered. "Some kids need help with their math facts. Others with reading or writing or following directions. Some just can't seem to sit still to do their work, and need the attention of someone sitting with them."

"Kind of a study buddy," Howard commented.

Mr. Corby laughed. "Yup."

"I could help someone in gym," Andy said. "That's my best subject."

"Oh, come on. That is *not* what Mr. Corby meant," Maureen said.

"Now, wait a minute," Mr. Corby said. "What Andy said is perfectly fine."

Andy looked relieved. Maureen looked amazed.

"Once we've got our list of younger students who need help, I'll be meeting with each of you to talk about what you will be doing," Mr. Corby said. "And there's one more thing; it's important to understand that we must respect these students, and not talk badly about them. We want to help, not make their problems worse."

Not make their problems worse, I repeated in my mind. Could I, Bently Barker, help some little kid with a problem, without making it worse? I wasn't doing so hot with my own problems, so how was I going to show anyone else what to do? Maybe I could just show what *not* to do, starting with *not* calling the biggest kid in the school a slime ball.

15.
The Fatal Disease

At four-thirty that afternoon I was lying on the couch with Farful. The television was on, but I was thinking more than I was watching. It was a relief to be temporarily safe from Anthony. If I had to share one skill right now with my new little study buddy, I could teach how to dodge and dart through the school without getting beaten up.

The telephone rang. I heard Colleen pick it up in her room. "Whhaatt!" she shrieked.

I wondered what the excitement was about.

"He told people *what*?" Colleen screeched. "I don't believe he did that. Probably for attention. He's gonna get it."

I scratched Farful behind her ear, glad that for once this week, someone *else* was "gonna get it." Probably one of her boyfriends.

"That is *soooo* low," Colleen went on. "I don't believe him." There was a thud upstairs. I knew Colleen threw something. That's what she always does when she's angry.

I pushed the button on the remote control to raise the volume on the television. Maybe I could drown out Colleen.

"*BENNNTLYYY!*"

Nope. I couldn't drown out Colleen.

"Get up here *right* now!" Colleen ordered.

Me? "Aw, come on. Give me a break," I muttered. But I got up. Farful padded behind me as I walked slowly up the stairs. "What?"

I peered into Colleen's room and found her sitting ramrod straight on the edge of her bed. She was clenching her fists and scowling angrily at me. "*You pea brain!* How could you do that? What is your problem?"

"Which one? I have about a million — "

Colleen cut me off. "I can't believe what I just heard from Kathy, who just heard from her sister that you've been telling people that you're dying. What kind of stupid thing is that to say? Huh?"

I stared at her for a minute. "What?" I finally said, my voice cracking.

"You heard me. There are easier ways to get attention," she said. "I am *so embarrassed*. I'm going to have to explain to everyone that you made that up."

"I went to the nurse today. That's all I did," I started to explain.

"That is *not* all you did, twerp. Kathy said her sister heard from Louie that you can't even walk right anymore and you don't have long to live," Colleen said.

"But I didn't mean . . . you know Louie, he takes everything seriously, he exaggerates. . . ." I remembered the time Louie told the class that he was having an operation almost as serious as a heart transplant. It turned out that he'd had a wart taken off his knee.

"You're gonna get it, Bently. I'm going to make *sure* you can't walk right. Wait till Mom and Dad hear about this."

Maybe I wouldn't get through the whole day without being beaten up, after all.

Farful slinked away toward my room to escape Colleen's loud voice. A moment later I heard Farful crawl under my bed. I thought about joining her and never coming out.

Dad was more understanding than Colleen thought he ought to be. "I'm humiliated," she said. "He is such a jerk for doing that!"

"It was not done on purpose, Colleen," Dad said, "and it certainly was not done to annoy you. Bently, not you, is the one who will have most of the explaining to do."

Colleen stalked off to her room. Soon after, she began belting out the song "I Heard It Through the Grapevine."

I left the house to take Farful for a walk before

dinner. I had to go a whole block to get away from Colleen's voice. Crossing the street to the park, I thought about all the food I had gotten at lunchtime. Maybe I shouldn't be too quick to tell people I'm not dying.

I got to thinking. It was just possible my days of being average were over. I was the only kid in the fifth grade with a fatal disease. I was also the only one who was going to get creamed by Anthony Magliari. Things weren't going the way they were supposed to, but at least I was soon to be a legend. "Wow!" people would say. "There goes Bently Barker. What a shame. And he never even had a chance to reach his goal."

16.
Who What?

I was tugging Farful away from the telephone pole she was sniffing when I heard a bike coming from behind. "Hey, Bently," said a low voice. "I want to talk to you."

I turned slowly . . . and faced ANTHONY MAGLIARI.

Farful, ATTACK! I tried to send her a mind-to-mind message. Farful's mind didn't get it. She stood wagging her tail.

ATTACK, you obedience-school failure. Protect me, lunge, chase, *growl*, at least.

"Nice dog," Anthony commented. I couldn't tell if Anthony was mocking me or if he really meant it. Farful didn't care. She practically smiled at him.

I stared at Anthony's forearms. They were twice the size of mine.

"Ummm . . ." Anthony shifted on the seat of his black bike. "Ahhh . . . I have to talk to you." He flexed his biceps. I wondered if he pumped iron or if they just naturally grew that way. "Someone told me . . ."

Oh, no. I winced. Here it comes. Be brave.

I backed up a step. It wouldn't matter in the end, but it might make the first punch a little easier to take.

"Ummm . . . someone said . . ." Anthony started again, ". . . that, ah, maybe . . ." He scuffed at the dirt with his sneaker.

Let's get this over with, Anthony, I thought. Yes, I called you a slime ball. Yes, I admit it.

"Well, you have a sister, right?" asked Anthony.

I nodded. What, was he going to get Colleen, too?

"Does she talk to you much?"

"Huh?" What did he want? For Colleen to talk to me about not calling people "slime ball"?

Anthony repeated the question. "Does she talk to you much?"

I shrugged. "Some."

"About any guys?" Anthony asked.

"What?"

"Guys. Does she talk about any?"

"I don't know. Sometimes . . . I guess." I wished Anthony would just get it over with and hit me.

"Who?" Anthony asked.

"Who what?"

"Who does she talk about?"

I rubbed my head. "I'm not sure. I don't listen."

"Oh. But maybe . . . uh, maybe you'd help me out."

Help him out? I felt like sticking a finger in my ear to see what was in there affecting my hearing.

"Maybe you could just say something," Anthony said.

I stared at him, wondering if this whole weird conversation was a trick to put me off guard. Then I thought that maybe Howard was right about the Twinkies — maybe they really were doing something to my brain. If I lived past this moment, I'd have to warn my little study buddy about that.

"To your sister . . . uh, could you . . . ummm maybe talk to her?" Anthony asked. He reached down and patted Farful.

"My *sister? Colleen?* Talk to her about what?"

"Me. But I guess you don't think I'm her type, right?"

I started to smile a little . . . then a lot. The relief was too much. I had to practically stuff my fist in my mouth to keep from laughing uncontrollably.

Anthony looked puzzled, then angry. "Hey — what? Something funny?"

"Nope," I said quickly.

Anthony continued. "Good, so how about you ask her what she thinks of me. And then you could say something good about me."

It was hard for me not to collapse on to the

ground in relief and throw grass into the air. Anthony was after Colleen, not me!

"Okay?" Anthony looked at me. "You'll talk to her?"

I looked back at Anthony. Not Anthony the Headless Horseman, or Anthony the giant, but Anthony the boy with a thing for my sister. A regular guy — well, maybe with terrible taste in girls, but still a regular guy.

"Okay," I said. "I'll say something for you. Anything special you want?"

"That I'm good-looking and cool," Anthony answered, grinning. He pulled a comb from the back pocket of his tight jeans and swept it through his thick, dark hair.

I smiled back. "Right."

"Thanks. Check you later," said Anthony, pushing off on his bike. He circled back. "Oh, and Bently . . . uh . . . I hear you're sick and all, right? So, could you do it soon?"

17.
A Brother–Sister Chat

The phone was ringing as I walked in my house. My father answered it. "Bently," he yelled.

"Yup!" I called. "Coming." I went down to the family room to talk.

"Bent? It's Howard. I know about the weirdness in school. My sister heard all about it."

"Seems everyone's sister heard, including mine," I answered. "Sisters have ears like Dumbo."

"It's pretty funny, really . . . unless, of course . . . I mean, you aren't actually sick or anything, are you?"

"Nope." I explained about Louie.

"Well, it wasn't really your fault, Bent. Louie gets awfully excited and worked up over illness and injury. He's a medical maniac."

I went on to tell about Anthony. Howard laughed so hard that I had to hold the phone away from my ear. When Howard finally calmed down, he said, "Now, all you have to do is tell people you aren't about to keel over."

After dinner I went into Colleen's room. Without even looking up from her magazine, she said, "OUT!" If I hadn't promised Anthony I'd talk to her, I'd have gladly stayed out. But a promise was a promise.

I stood there for a minute, and she kept ignoring me. Finally, I flicked her lights off and on a couple times to get her attention.

"Cut it out, Twit. And don't even *think* of trying that idiot truck charge again with the flashlights."

"Okay. How's school?"

She looked at me suspiciously. "Why?"

"Just wondered," I said, stepping into her room.

"After that dumb thing you did today, I don't know why I'm even talking to you. But I'll tell you this much — seventh grade isn't like the baby grades. We switch rooms *every* period and get a *lot* of different teachers, not just one," she said importantly.

I wondered about having more than one teacher. Would I need goals for each of them?

I tried to keep our talk going and steer it toward Anthony. "Ummm, who do you have in your classes?"

"Some of my friends, but not all. A lot of the fun kids are in other sections," Colleen said, sighing. She reached for a fingernail file and began filing.

Maybe Anthony was one of those fun kids. I'd try to find out by sneaking in Anthony's name with some others. "Like Bryan Rosen? Or Ronnie Ogden? Or Anthony Magliari? Hey, I'll bet Anthony is a really fun guy, heh-heh," I said, trying to chuckle a little as I said it.

The filing stopped. Colleen's surprised face turned red. "What are you getting at, Bently? Did you hear something?"

"Me? No, why?"

"Come *on*, Bently. What did you hear?"

"Nothing. Brothers don't hear much. Only sisters hear things." But I remembered when I saw Anthony at the teachers' room door when I'd gone to get octopus food. Anthony had mumbled something about his girl. That girl had to be Colleen.

"What's to hear?" I asked innocently.

"You tell *me*, Nerf-brain. You know something."

I looked as blank as I could. "What would I know?"

"Oh, you are being so . . . oh, all right. But you better not tell Mom and Dad," Colleen said.

"Okay."

"Well, there was this fight," Colleen explained. "Mom and Dad hate fighting. So don't tell."

"I won't, I won't. What happened?"

"Anthony hit Buford Amos because Buford said

something about my singing," Colleen explained. "They both got in trouble."

"Oh." I figured it had been something like that. "So, what do you think of Anthony? He seems like an okay guy. I mean, he did stick up for you and all."

Colleen looked down at her lap and fiddled with a thread on her jeans. "Ummm . . . sometimes it gets hard . . . you know . . . to like all the kids you want to like."

"Oh." I wasn't sure what Colleen meant.

"I mean, when you get older, it's really dumb how careful kids get about who they hang out with. You'll see, in a couple of years." She looked up at me.

I nodded. I hadn't had a talk with Colleen in a long time. It felt sort of good to be having one now, even if I wasn't sure what she was talking about.

"Anthony isn't in the group I'm with," Colleen said, "but he's nice — at least he's nice to me."

"Don't kids like him?" I asked.

"Yeah, but most of my friends don't know him very well. He spends a lot of time with eighth graders, because he used to be in the same grade as that group. He's not dumb, but he had trouble learning to read. At least that's what I heard. He reads fine now."

"Soooo . . ." I said.

"Soooo . . ." she repeated. "Why the questions, anyway?"

I shrugged. "No reason."

"I don't believe you," she said suspiciously. "You haven't come in this room to talk in ages. What are you up to?"

"Nothing. It's just good to know what to expect in school in a couple of years. I *thought* I knew what to expect this year, but it's nothing like I thought." I backed through the door. I couldn't ask any more about Anthony.

"Hold it, Bent. How'd the thing with the bracelet go?" Colleen grinned. "Hmmm? Did you give it to the girl?"

"No."

"Ohhh — " Colleen sounded sorry. "What happened?"

"Nothing. I just didn't give it to her. You can have it back."

She nodded and picked up her nail file. "Okay."

I fished the bracelet out of my pocket, glad to be rid of it. There were two Jujubes stuck to it. Colleen didn't look so glad to have it back.

I was partway to my room when I heard Colleen call, "I *still* think you should have gotten into more trouble than you did, twerp-face, for making people think you're practically dead. You better tell the truth on Monday."

It was too early for bed, so I just poked around

in my room, ate some stale peanut butter crackers, and put things in piles for a while. I always do that when I'm bored. I had piles of baseball cards, sports magazines, books, miniature golf score cards, plastic pouches of catsup from McDonald's. Howard and I have a special use for the catsup — we put it under the tires of parked cars and then watch it splatter when the cars roll over it.

I took Ruckles out of his bowl. Ruckles exercises by walking around my floor. "Turtle trotting," I call it.

While Ruckles trotted, I looked at a magic book Dad gave me last year. Maybe it would explain how to make a fatal disease magically disappear.

I thought about my little study buddy — poor kid, getting matched up with Bently the mess-up. At least I'd have something else to tell the kid not to do. Do *not* discuss your troubles or your health with a person like Louie.

"Time to hit the spray," I told Ruckles as I put him back in his bowl and splashed a bit of water over his shell. "Be glad you have a nice safe place here. All you have to think about is your bowl, not your goal."

18.
The Confession

"WHAT!" Maureen shrieked, slapping the bus seat as we bounced along to school Monday morning. "You're *not* sick? I'm going to kill you, Bently!" Her nostrils flared.

Howard and I grinned back at her.

"Fit as a Fig Newton," I said.

"Yup, Bently's so healthy, he could make vitamin commercials," Howard added.

"That was a lousy thing to do and you know it," Maureen shot back, glaring at me. "It's settled now. Anthony Magliari and I are having a chat." She leaned back in her seat and folded her hands across her chest. "*Today.*"

"You're too late, Maureen," I told her. "Anthony and I already talked."

"Yup," Howard chimed in, "they're pals now."

"Ha, that's impossible. No way." Maureen shook her head.

Louie sat nine rows ahead of us. I think he could

hear Maureen's loud voice, but probably couldn't tell what was going on. He looked surprised to see me looking so well.

When we got to school, Anthony was waiting for me.

"I'll meet you on the field in a few minutes," I said to Howard. Then I walked to where Anthony was leaning against the bike rack.

"I did it. I talked to Colleen for you," I said.

Anthony waited. "Yeah? What'd she say?"

"That you're nice."

Anthony smiled a little. "Yeah?"

"And that you stuck up for her," I added.

Anthony nodded and looked as if he were waiting for more.

"That's kind of it. It was a pretty short talk."

"That's okay." Anthony looked down at my sneakers and grinned. Then he walked off whistling.

I wished I could have told Anthony something else, or done something more . . . something that might make up for calling him a slime ball.

On my way past Maureen, I heard her mutter, "What was that all about? What's going on?"

Until it was time to go inside, Willie and I took turns trying to kick a soccer ball past Howard, who was practicing his goalie skills.

"You've got guts," Willie said to me as we

walked from the field toward the building when the bell rang.

"What?"

"Guts. You've got 'em," Willie repeated.

I stood trying to figure out what gutsy thing I'd done. Talked to Anthony?

"You know," Willie went on, "playing even though you're so sick."

I felt my face turning red. "Oh, well, you see, I'm okay, really. Not that sick. Not even half-sick, actually. . . ."

"You're tough, Bently. Way to go." Willie patted me on the back and jogged off to pick up his books. I stood there still trying to get the right words out.

"You've got to tell them, Bent," Howard said, wiping his glasses on his shirt. "Straight out."

I did. At nine-fifteen Mr. Corby had to go to the office to get paper. When he left the room, I stood up and cleared my throat. "Hey, everyone. Listen up."

They looked up . . . and waited. I stared at them for a while without speaking. Finally I began. "Uh, this is kind of hard to say. . . ." My face felt sweaty and blotchy.

Lisa, Kathryn, and Maria all nodded kindly.

I went on. "Some people heard something . . . um, something about a disease." I glanced at Louie, who quickly looked down and began picking at some tape on his desk.

Howard mouthed, "Hurry up," and gestured in the direction of the office. Mr. Corby would be back soon.

"You don't have to talk about it if you don't want to," Lisa said softly. She fingered one of her rainbow erasers, then looked up at me with sad eyes.

"*Yes*, he does," Maureen hissed. "You tell them, Bently. *Now*." She tapped her pencil on her desk while she waited. Then she muttered, "They didn't believe *me*."

I cleared my throat again. "Well, this disease isn't really so bad. . . ." I saw Howard shaking his head. "No, I mean, I said the wrong thing to Louie, and he misunderstood."

"You're brave," Kathryn said.

"Very." Lisa nodded.

"Thank you," I said. Howard shook his head again, and Maureen let out a snort.

"I mean I'm totally okay. Not sick. Fine," I said.

"How fine?" asked Andy.

"Well . . . very. Uh, very fine," I answered.

Louie blurted out, "But you *said* you had some sort of nerve problem. *And* not long to live."

"I didn't mean it the way it sounded," I explained. "Sorry. It was actually a *lack* of nerve problem. I'll live."

Louie mumbled, "I don't get it."

I answered, "Right, that's why I have to be up here straightening things out, Lou."

"Phony faker Bentbrain *Barfer*'s a fraud," snarled Maureen.

I stepped toward Maureen. "Not on purpose. So butt out of my business." Wow, I surprised myself with that one.

I guess I surprised a lot of other people, too. Kids began to smile. A few even clapped.

Maureen sputtered.

Lisa looked at me and said, "I'm glad you're okay."

I think my freckles lit up like Christmas lights.

Mr. Corby's footsteps ended the discussion.

As the class settled down, I heard Maureen say, "Oh, shoot, he's really going to live. I had my outfit picked out for the funeral."

19.
Study Buddies

"Goal time," Mr. Corby announced. Desk tops went up, and we pulled out our goal books. It hadn't taken long before goal time had become pretty popular. Some of the kids had started talking about their goals to each other, and most had shared with Mr. Corby. Not me.

Mr. Corby handed back goal books to the kids who'd turned them in. I watched as one by one the kids opened them and read what Mr. Corby had written. Kathryn peeked quickly at hers, smiled, then put it in her desk. Maria looked nervous before she opened her book, but finally she read what Mr. Corby had written. Maria looked relieved. Howard laughed out loud and then picked up his pen and wrote something underneath Mr. Corby's comment.

Willie and Andy had both been watching Howard. "I'm handing mine in tomorrow," Willie said.

"Me, too," Andy agreed.

Maybe I'd hand in my book soon, too. If other

kids could tell their goals, I ought to be able to.

I could see that Louie's goal to grow wasn't happening very fast. Maybe there was some way to stretch him to speed things up. But after what Louie did, telling everyone I was dying, he deserved to be shrunk.

Howard was whiz-reading his way toward his goal of getting through the "H" volume of *World Book Encyclopedia*. He'd get way past that goal by June and would probably start writing his own encyclopedia.

"It's time to talk about our study-buddy program," Mr. Corby said. "I now have my list of younger students needing help, and I think you're settled enough into fifth grade to be ready to begin. I'm going to call each of you up to my desk this afternoon. We'll talk about your big buddy match-ups."

I watched as kids sat in the chair next to Mr. Corby's desk and talked with him. When it was my turn, I felt nervous. What if I didn't know enough to teach someone?

"You will be working with a six-year-old named Leon. He's in Ms. Watson's class." Mr. Corby opened a folder and showed me two papers that Leon had worked on. "You see, Leon has trouble with his letters. He switches some of them around."

I looked at a sentence Leon had tried to copy. "The dog saw the bird" was copied, "The bog saw the dirb."

"Ms. Watson will explain what you can do to help Leon," Mr. Corby said. "Leon already gets some extra help from Mrs. Sanchez, the reading skills teacher, but Ms. Watson thinks that a lot of what Leon needs is practice and encouragement. That's where you come in."

I sat down in my bus seat that afternoon and looked out the window. I saw my sister talking with Anthony by the bike rack.

Howard stumbled down the aisle dragging his backpack full of books. He collapsed into the seat next to me.

"Look at that." I pointed to Colleen climbing onto the back of Anthony's bike.

"Oh, yeah," said Howard. "Colleen said to tell you she wasn't coming home on the bus. She has a ride."

"She sure does," I said, watching them ride away.

"I don't know about you, but I'm going to do some planning tonight," Howard said. "Tomorrow we start working with our study buddies. Mine's name is Duncan and he goes to Mr. Lewis the period before I do."

"He goes to *Mr. Lewis*, the teacher who works with brainy kids like you?" I asked.

Howard nodded.

"Then how could he need help? I thought we

were working with kids who were having trouble in school?"

Howard sighed impatiently. "We are. Bent, do you think smart kids have no problems? Do you think having brains is all there is to it?"

I considered saying yes, but didn't.

Howard went on. "This kid, Duncan, may be one of the smartest people in the school. But he has trouble getting his thoughts down on paper. He also doesn't know how to talk to other kids."

I told Howard about Leon. "He might need a lot of help." I wondered if Mr. Corby had picked the right person for the job. "I just hope I don't confuse him more."

When Colleen got home, she waved as she passed my doorway on her way down the hall to her room. "Hey, brother Bent."

"Hey, yourself." I grinned at her. "How was your ride home?"

Colleen looked embarrassed. "Great." She walked away singing, "A Bicycle Built for Two."

After lunch the next day, Mr. Corby announced that it was time for the class to go meet their little buddies. My stomach flip-flopped as I walked downstairs toward Ms. Watson's room.

When I opened the first-grade classroom door, everyone inside the room turned and looked at me.

Ms. Watson was seated at a small table talking

with four students. She stood up and walked over to me. "Hello, I'm happy to have you come to our class, Bently. Let me introduce you to Leon." She looked toward a boy sitting at a desk right next to hers. "Leon, I want you to meet someone."

I didn't think Leon looked as happy to see me as Ms. Watson did. Maybe he doesn't want help, I thought. Maybe he thinks I should mind my own business. I ought to leave.

Ms. Watson smiled at us. "I have a table and some chairs set outside in the hall. That would be a quiet place to work." She patted Leon on the shoulder. "Leon, you may get your reading papers from your desk. Take them and a pencil to the table in the hall."

I wasn't sure whether to follow Leon or to wait for Ms. Watson to tell me what to do.

"Bently, it would be helpful to Leon if you would look at his work with him. Help him stay with the task." She smiled. "He has trouble sitting still and finishing. Your attention will make a difference."

I nodded and went out into the hall where Leon was waiting. I wanted to say something great. I stood looking down at Leon. Should I do what most teachers do the first day? Talk about bathroom rules and drink a cup of coffee?

Leon glanced up at me. Then he picked up his pencil.

He's going to start without me, I thought. Wait. "Leon, let's talk about your goals."

20.
Leon

Leon stared up at me. "It's good to have a goal, Leon. That way you know where you are going."

"I'm not supposed to go anywhere," Leon said. "I'm supposed to sit here."

"I know. But what do you want this year? What would you like to see happen?" Oh, no, I sounded just like Warren.

Leon didn't answer. He probably didn't know what I was talking about. The poor kid must think he got the booby prize of big buddies.

"Well," I said. "I think one goal I probably had in first grade was to have recess." I grinned at Leon.

"Mostly I have to finish my work at recess," Leon said.

"Okay, then. We'll try to get it done on time. Then you'll have recess." I decided that might be enough of a goal for Leon. We worked for a few minutes, and then Leon was up. He wandered to

103

the other side of the hall and peered into a classroom.

"Leon, over here. You need to finish this," I said.

Leon looked into another classroom.

"Leon, come on, sit. I'll help you. Look, we have to fix this word. You wrote 'dat' instead of 'bat.' "

I got Leon back in his seat, but in a few more minutes he was up again. When Ms. Watson came out to tell us that time was up, I was worn out. I had no idea that working with little kids could be so hard. It always seemed to me that teachers pretty much just told kids what to do. I never knew that some kids had to be chased to get them to do it.

On my way back to my classroom, I met Lisa. "How'd your buddy session go?" I asked. My voice sounded wiggly.

"Pretty good," Lisa answered. "My little buddy is a second grader named Karen. She reminds me of myself."

"How?" I asked.

"She's into dancing, and gymnastics, and piano," Lisa said. "She's doing a lot."

"What are you helping her with?"

"Math. But I think it will turn out to be more."

"Why do you think that?" I asked. I wondered if I should be thinking of more to help Leon with.

"Karen doesn't really like all the extra things she's doing," Lisa explained. "She loves gymnastics, but not really everything else. It's her parents who like those things."

"How can you help her with that?" We were almost to our classroom.

"I'm kind of working on a problem like that myself. Mr. Corby knows about it, but no one else . . . except you, now." Lisa looked away.

I never knew she had a problem. "You have to do activities you don't like? Like what?" We stopped by the water fountain.

"Well, one thing mainly. And it's not that I don't like it at all. I just don't love it the way my mother wants me to."

"Love what?" I leaned over and took a drink.

"The violin. She wants me to be a serious violinist. But I don't like violin that much and I'm not very good. Dancing is what I really like."

"Can't you tell her?" I asked, wiping my mouth with the back of my hand.

"Ha. You don't know Mom," Lisa said.

I popped two Jujubes into my mouth. "Want one?"

"No thanks."

"Hey, what's up, Bent, my man." Anthony Magliari walked toward us. "Slap me five."

I reached out and slapped Anthony five, while a surprised-looking Lisa watched.

"You taking a little break from class?" Anthony grinned.

I swallowed the Jujubes. I couldn't take the

chance that I might accidentally spit them at Anthony. "Well, we're — "

"Don't rush back, take your time." He looked down at my sneakers and gave the thumbs up sign. "See you later, pal." Anthony leaned over the water fountain and took a long, slow drink. Then he sauntered down the hall.

Lisa looked at me, then back to where Anthony was disappearing around the corner. "Wow. Isn't he the toughest kid in the school?"

I shrugged and answered, "Yeah."

"Guess he doesn't bother you, though," she said.

"Nope," I said, trying to sound as cool as possible.

Lisa smiled. "Well, probably we'd better go back now."

Maureen looked up as Lisa and I walked into the room. "Well, you two took your time getting back here."

"We stopped to get a drink," Lisa answered. "Then — get this, everybody — Anthony Magliari called Bently 'pal,' and slapped him five."

I walked toward my desk, moving in the slow, cool way Anthony did.

"*What?*" Maureen exclaimed.

"Pal," Howard said. "You know, as in: friend, ally, buddy, chum . . ."

"And slapped him five?" Louie murmured.

"Slapped five," Howard continued, "as in: 'greetings, cool buddy,' 'way to go, slick dude,' 'great seeing you, Bently, my man'..."

Things were looking up.

21.
Someone's in the Kitchen

A few days later when I walked into Leon's class, Leon had his head in his desk.

"Leon will be with you in a minute, Bently," Ms. Watson said. "He needs to find some papers." She paused for a moment, then said, "But I have an idea. Why don't we just move the desk to the hall and let you help Leon get organized. Show him how to put things where he can find them."

If Ms. Watson could see my own black-hole desk, she'd change her mind about this idea.

Once Leon's desk was in the hall, we began. "Okay, let's take everything out. We can stack things on the table here," I said.

Leon scooped up some crayons and an eraser and handed them to me. Next came some broken pretzels, a straw, a dead beetle, and a reading book. Leon was pulling out some crumpled papers, when he looked up and smiled.

"Hi, Anthony," Leon said.

"Bently — you helping my pal, Leon?" Anthony asked.

I nodded. "Trying to."

"Well, good. Leon, you listen to my buddy, Bently." Anthony ruffled Leon's hair and smiled. "So long."

When Anthony disappeared around the corner, I asked, "You know Anthony?"

"Yup. Sometimes on weekends he shows me how to skateboard."

I couldn't believe I ever thought this little buddy might need advice about handling the big guys.

I tried to smooth out the papers Leon was pulling from the desk. On the top of one paper, "NOEL" was written where "LEON" should have been. Merry Christmas, Leon.

On another paper, where Leon's name should have been, was "LONE."

"I don't know if I'm a good enough big buddy to Leon," I said to Howard after school. "The little guy is so mixed up."

"A lot of people are, Bent," Howard said. "My little buddy, Duncan, is so smart in some ways, but doesn't know the first thing about a lot of ordinary things. Seven out of ten people — "

"Hold it, Howard. Leon and Duncan are people, not numbers."

Howard thought for a moment. "Yeah. You're right."

I walked home from the bus stop, feeling guilty that I'd grumbled the first day of school about being in middle groups. Lone Leon was probably altogether groupless. And that was nothing to sing "Noel" about.

I stopped short when I saw that Anthony was in the kitchen with Colleen. They were sticking spoons into a jar of peanut butter.

"Hey, Bent," Anthony said.

I couldn't believe that only a short time ago I'd been positive that this very cool person, who was now eating my peanut butter, was going to beat me to mush.

"So, what was going on in the hall by Ms. Watson's room?" Anthony asked. "Are you helping her or something?"

"Everyone in my class is helping a littler kid in the school. Leon is the one I'm working with."

"I had Ms. Watson in first grade . . . twice," Anthony said. "My parents say she's a saint. When Ms. Watson asked to hold me back, she also asked to have me in her class again."

I tried to imagine Anthony back then. He must have been like the little Elvis of the first grade.

"I had a slow start," Anthony said. "But I caught up. I bet Leon will, too."

Colleen gave me a look. I knew she wanted me

out of the room, but I didn't want to go so soon. It was great having Anthony in my kitchen, talking to me like a buddy.

I poured a drink and sat down, figuring I'd push my luck just a little. But Colleen repeated the look, this time with eyes so fierce that I grabbed my drink and beat it out of there.

I flopped on my bed and stared at the marks on my ceiling. Howard and I used to throw Silly Putty up there, and then we'd time how long it would stick.

I thought about Leon and Anthony and me, and about how the year was turning out — not the way I'd expected. I reached over the side of my bed and pulled my goal book from my backpack. I sighed and read over my first goal. Then I picked up a pencil and wrote:

I don't Know whether I'm ever going to be outstanding, but at least maybe I can help Leon. Just getting through everything is a lot for any kid.

22.
Wonder Buddy

The big-buddy sessions soon became a regular part of the day for Mr. Corby's class. Mr. Corby had conferences with each of us to see how things were going. When he talked with me, he had some ideas to help keep Leon sitting and working. Small rewards would help, Mr. Corby said.

I tried that suggestion. I used some stickers from one of my collections. Leon liked those and tried hard to earn them. He stayed in his seat more, but he still had some problems with switching letters around. Finally I came up with a way to help Leon get his name right each time.

"Just remember this: Leon — *Leap Easily Over Nerds.*"

"What?" Leon looked up and laughed. "Why?"

"So you can get the letters in your name in the right order," I explained, and pointed to the L, E, O, N.

Leon laughed. "Okay." He repeated, "Leap

easily over nerds. Got it." He got his name right every time after that. I was beginning to feel like Wonder Buddy.

Next, we attacked Leon's problem with "d" and "b" mix-up. But it wasn't easy. I tried to draw pictures — like a duck with the body of a "d"; the trouble was that if that duck turned around, it would have the body of a "b."

Finally, I decided to ask Mr. Corby for help. A teacher ought to know about these things. I explained about Leon's problem in my goal book. On my way out the door to go home, I put the goal book on Mr. Corby's desk.

Later I spent the night thinking and worrying. I remembered that my goal about wanting to be outstanding was in the goal book, right there in plain sight. And worse, my second, third, fourth, and fifth goals, which I'd meant to rip out, were still there. Warren would think I was a wimp, writing about things like my green sneakers, my fear of killing Archie (and the other way around), my pants, and my dumb panic about Anthony.

Maybe Mr. Corby hadn't taken the goal book home. I could sneak back to school and snatch it off Mr. Corby's desk. But the doors would probably be locked at nine o'clock at night. If I tried to climb in a window, alarms might go off. I could picture a swarm of police cars surrounding me, cameras flashing, and my picture on the front page of every newspaper the next morning. So much for the sneak-and-snatch plan.

There was always a chance that Mr. Corby wouldn't have time to read the goal book. He might be busy with his animals, or with scuba diving, or with a huge feast of desserts and licorice.

In the morning, the first thing I did when I got to my classroom was look for my goal book. It wasn't on Mr. Corby's desk where I'd left it. Not a good sign.

Just as I was trying to decide if I dared look through the things on the desk, Mr. Corby walked into the room. He set his thermos down on the desk and then began to unpack his briefcase. Out came some spelling papers, a stack of math tests, and three goal books.

Thinking that there still might be a chance that Mr. Corby hadn't looked at the goal books yet, I stepped up to the desk. "Excuse me, may I have that back?" I asked, pointing to my book.

Mr. Corby looked at me and smiled. "Sure." He handed it to me.

Walking back to my desk, I flipped through the book. Too late. Mr. Corby had seen everything — and he'd written some comments. I sat down and began to read.

Next to my goal about wanting to be outstanding, not boring, Mr. Corby had written:

> BORING IS NOT SOMETHING YOU'LL
> EVER BE. YOUR BENTLY-NESS
> WILL NEVER ALLOW IT.

Beside my goal about wanting to be known for my outstanding feats, not my outstanding feet, Mr. Corby had said:

> I'M GUESSING THAT YOUR
> "OUTSTANDING FEET" HAS TO
> DO WITH YOUR A-1, VERY
> ORIGINAL SNEAKERS. THEY
> REALLY HAVE "SOLE."

After my goal about not wanting to be Bloody Bently the Octopus Murderer, Warren had put:

> ARCHIE'S FINE - NEVER LOOKED
> BETTER. YOU DID A GREAT
> JOB FEEDING HIM.

The comment next to my goal not to get out of my chair was:

> DOES THIS HAVE ANYTHING
> TO DO WITH YOUR OUTSTANDING
> SEAT ? (I DON'T MEAN TO
> MAKE IT THE BUTT OF ANY
> JOKES.)

Below my wish to make a name for myself and then stay alive to enjoy it, was written:

> YOU APPEAR TO BE ALIVE
> AND WELL AND DOING GREAT,
> BENTLY. KEEP IT UP.

Finally, by my statement about wanting to help Leon, Warren had written:

YOU'RE RIGHT. GETTING
THROUGH EVERYTHING IS A
LOT FOR A KID. AND THAT'S
ONE REASON WE'RE DOING
THIS BIG BUDDY PROJECT.
STOP AND SEE ME BEFORE
YOU GO TO LUNCH. I HAVE A
COUPLE OF IDEAS THAT MAY
HELP WITH LEON'S "b" AND "d"
PROBLEM.   MR. C.

I was glad I'd finally turned in my goal book. Warren hadn't commented on my wimpiness at all. In fact, he'd been pretty nice.

On my way to lunch, I stopped at Mr. Corby's desk.

"I've thought about Leon's problem," Mr. Corby said. "Here's what I've come up with." He took out a piece of paper and began to draw.

First he showed how a lowercase "b" looks like an uppercase "B," except that the top bump isn't there.

"Oh, yeah. Right," I said. Why hadn't I thought of that?

"Now for the 'd' — I thought of something kind of funny," Mr. Corby said. "But I'll bet Leon will remember it." Mr. Corby drew a "d" and then turned it into a stick figure of a person with a large rear end.

"Okay, now there is a French word for one's behind or rear end — it's *'derrière.'*" Mr. Corby wrote the word down. I thought it would be spelled "dairy air," the way it sounded.

"If you draw this figure for Leon and then teach him the word *'derrière,'* he should remember 'd.'" Mr. Corby grinned.

My face was red by this time, but I did think it was pretty funny that my teacher was teaching me the French word for rear end. It was turning out to be some weird year.

"Leon, I have something to show you," I said an hour later.

When I got to the *derrière* part, Leon started laughing. I tried to keep a teacher face, but lost it. We both started laughing. Ms. Watson stuck her head out the door and asked, "How's the work coming? Are you getting it done?"

"Uh-huh," I said, nodding. "We're doing fine." I held my breath to keep from laughing. As soon as the door closed, we both spluttered and started in again.

Trying to do what Mr. Corby had done, I drew the "d" stick figure, and then said, "I forget exactly how you spell the French word, but that doesn't matter."

Just before Leon and I finished for the afternoon, Anthony came down the hall on his way to the water fountain. "Hey, Anthony," Leon called. "Look at this." Laughing, Leon drew the "d" stick person and explained about *derrière*.

Anthony put one arm around Leon's shoulder, and the other around mine. "Wow, you're a lucky dude, Leon. My man Bently is a marvel."

23.
Some Year

"So how are we doing?" Mr. Corby asked the class. "We've got a few minutes before lunch. Let's talk about the buddy program. You've been doing it for a few weeks now. Any thoughts?"

"Yeah," Andy said. "Teaching isn't all that easy."

"But it's fun," Patty added. "I really like it. Maybe becoming a teacher could be my goal for when I'm older."

"I couldn't do it," Louie said. "Little kids cough and sneeze right at you. Too many germs."

"No way for me, either," Maureen said. "Some of these kids have attitudes."

"It takes one to know one," Howard whispered.

"The kid I'm working with keeps saying, 'This stinks,' " Maureen went on.

Howard mumbled, "You heard it wrong, Maureen. The kid said, '*You* stink.' "

If Mr. Corby heard Howard, he didn't let on. "Is the attitude improving, Maureen?"

"I guess so," she admitted. "He only says 'This stinks' every ten minutes now, instead of every five."

"Good, and how's the math coming along?" Mr. Corby asked.

"Fine," Maureen admitted. "He got a star on his last paper." She looked proud.

The bell for lunch rang. As Mr. Corby stood up, he knocked over the coffee cup on his desk. "Ooops," he said. "Maybe we'll have to postpone the spelling test until these papers dry."

The class cheered and applauded.

Warren, you really need to think about a klutz-improvement goal, I thought. Think about how many of your ties and shirts, not to mention your students' papers, are spotted with coffee, licorice, or tomato sauce. On second thought, the spilling isn't important. It's just a part of your Warren-ness.

Mopping his desk, Mr. Corby said, "We have an assembly program in the auditorium this afternoon. So, no goal talk today. But here's an idea. Next week let's plan a 'Going for the Goal' party."

More cheers and applause.

At recess, I saw Lisa sitting on the bench near the bike rack. She was writing. I wasn't sure whether I ought to bother her. I decided I'd be able to tell if she didn't want to talk.

"Hi," I said.

Lisa looked up and smiled. "Hi, Bently."

That sounded friendly enough, so I continued, "I was just wondering how things were going."

Lisa drew a happy face on the back of her goal book and held it up. "Things are going great. I did it. I finally talked to my mother about the violin. At first I think maybe she was disappointed. But the more we talked about how I feel about dancing, the better she seemed to be about it."

"That's great."

"I think I even convinced my mom that *she's* the one who should take violin lessons. It's not too late for her to learn."

"Right." I could see that Lisa was relieved. "Someday maybe I'll watch you dance." I couldn't believe I just said that.

"Really? You'd come to a performance?" Lisa asked.

"Sure I'd come." I couldn't believe I just added *that* to what I'd said before. But somehow I thought that seeing Lisa dance would be one of the nicest things ever, although I'd never say it out loud.

"Bently?" Lisa asked. "Sometime do you think you could help me make a pair of sneakers like yours?"

"Like these A-1, very original ones? Sure." I grinned. "I'd be a real heel if I said no."

Lisa groaned and pushed me a little.

Maybe this is what grown-ups mean when they talk about heart and sole.

Howard waved to me from the back of the bus. I sat down next to him and then leaned over to look for Jujubes in the pouch of my backpack. I heard someone plunk down in the seat next to us. Then I heard a familiar groan.

"Your *derrière* is on your bag, Maureen," I said.

Maureen whipped around in her seat. "Where'd you learn that word?"

"Why?" I asked.

"Good word, Bent," Howard commented. "Excellent word."

" 'Cause my stepbrother says it all the time. Twenty times a day," Maureen said. "He even called *me* a *derrière*. Of course, when my mother asked him if he said that, he told her he'd said I was a *dear*."

I had a sudden weird feeling. No, couldn't be. Not my cool little buddy, Lone Leon. But I had to ask. "Who is your stepbrother?"

"Leon. He's in first grade," she answered.

"Ohhh." I sagged in my seat. "Leon in *our* school?"

"Yup."

I couldn't believe it. "But then why isn't he on this bus with you?"

She sighed impatiently and added one of those

you-are-so-dumb looks. "He lives with us on week-ends. His father is married to my mother."

So that's how Leon knew Anthony. Same neighborhood.

I saw Maureen's expression change as she stared at me. "Wait a minute. Are *you* helping Leon? *You're* his big buddy?"

I nodded.

"That figures. That just figures. Thanks a heap. It's *your* fault he called me a *derrière*," Maureen said. "You're in for it now, Bently Barfer."

"What for? Leon's doing better, isn't he?"

Maureen looked surprised. She didn't answer right away. Finally she said, "Maybe you're doing a decent job . . . maybe."

Next to me, I could hear Howard saying, "Eighty percent of the kids who are mean and rotten to other kids eventually say something nice."

"*But* Leon's becoming a twerpy know-it-all pain. And if you *ever* teach him another one of those stupid French words he can use on me, you're *really* gonna get it."

"Then again," Howard added, "there are exceptions. Some people *never* say anything nice."

Maureen stood up, stuck her face in my face, squinted her eyes, and spat the words, "And I *mean* it."

As she marched down the aisle to another seat,

I whispered, "She said *French* words, Howie —
she didn't say anything about English, Spanish,
Italian, German . . ."

"Good thinking," Howard answered. "I've got
some foreign dictionaries at home. You can find
some more stuff to teach Leon."

What a cool challenge. General Bently and Lieu-
tenant Leon wage war on Maureen.

I leaned forward and pulled half of a leftover
peanut butter sandwich out of my backpack. I
opened the plastic bag, pulled off a piece of sandwich, and lobbed a glob toward Maureen's head.

"She didn't see that," Howard commented.

"She'll see the next one," I said, grinning.

Boy, I thought, as I pulled off another piece and
got ready to peg her with it, this was turning out
to be some year. A lot had happened since the
morning I flattened Howard's lunch. I learned a
few things, too — like that flattening sandwiches
isn't my only talent, and that getting through
everything is a lot like wading through peanut
butter . . . sometimes chunky, sometimes smooth.